Me'ansome

The Grave Knights
Book 1

International Bestselling Author
M. Merin

MOTORCYCLES, MAFIA, AND MAYHEM EVENT DISCLAIMER

This book is a work of fiction that was created as a multi-author collaboration to tie-in to a reader event and not a representation of actual events. I didn't get to mention every author I wanted to and thought it best to change the name of my—again—fictional readers who interact with my characters.

With that in mind, happy hunting! For books, happy hunting for books and new authors!

NOTE

In my first several RBMC, Flagstaff Chapter books, Joey's father's MC is referred to as the Hades Knights. I never planned on a spin-off, but in the years between me writing **Axel** and then starting this book for the MMM signing, that fictional title was used by another author and I decided to alter the name of Parker King's MC to avoid confusion. So, for those of you who were paying attention, remember this fictional world has to be fluid sometimes.

CHARACTER LIST

Characters previously introduced:

Parker King – road name Me'ansome which is a Cornish phrase - a mother's endearment for a male child. He has twins from a previous relationship.

Tin – Long time friend of Parker and VP of the Grave Knights.

Joey – Parker's daughter who was raised by her mother's family. Married to Axel Saint, of the Royal Bastards. (Axel: Royal Bastards MC, Flagstaff Chapter, Book 1)

Tommy/Ransom – Joey's twin brother who was raised by Parker.

Axel – VP of the RBMC, Flagstaff Chapter. (Axel: Royal Bastards MC, Flagstaff Chapter, Book 1)

Declan – President of the RBMC, Flagstaff Chapter. (Declan: Royal Bastards MC, Flagstaff Chapter, Book 2)

Red – Tin's older brother and a member of the RBMC, Flagstaff Chapter.

Diesel – IT and Security for the RBMC, Flagstaff Chapter and its holdings. (Diesel: Royal Bastards MC, Flagstaff Chapter, Book 3)

Wolfman – He handles wet work for the MC. (Wolfman: Royal Bastards MC, Flagstaff Chapter, Book 5)

New characters:

Piper Kyle – IT consultant with an identical twin sister that she covers for during MMM.

Paige Kyle - Self-published romance author, thief, and con-woman.

Rozzer – a Cornish term for cop.

Tober – Piper and Paige's cousin.

Felix – Tober, Piper, and Paige's cousin.

PROLOGUE

Parker King / Me'ansome - *Then*

"Fucking twins, man," I say, heavily exhaling as I get the news from my vice-president, Tin.

I've been on the road longer than I had planned and Jayne went into labor early. She's going to give me shit for the rest of my life for missing our babies' birth.

Damn. A boy and a girl, I think, grinning like a maniac.

Throwing my head back I holler, "Twins!" into the night as I start up my bike and get back on the road. It's only then that Tin's warning penetrates the euphoria of the news of my children's birth.

My Ol' Lady's a wild girl, I knew that well enough when I took up with her. Hell, it was my brother who rode in with her on the back of his bike one day—during one of the many breaks from his girl, Polly.

Jayne caught my eye the moment I saw her; just a fucking crazy-ass chick with an infectious laugh. We all knew she was from a very different background than most of the men and women involved in my fledgling motorcycle club; and for as *down and dirty* as she likes to act, I know her well enough to know she cringes when coasters aren't used.

Wherever the fuck Jayne came from don't matter to me, I know those babies are mine and getting home to them is all that matters.

I'm standing at the glass window outside the NICU when Tin walks up behind me.

"Where the fuck is she?" I growl out.

"Hell, if I know," he says, holding his hands up. "They were in a room with her when I left last night."

A man in scrubs walks toward me and does a double take when he takes in Tin and I standing outside a room with so many babies.

"Can I help you?" he asks, his eyes darting around, but not fixing onto either of us.

"Yeah, my girl gave birth yesterday. Jayne Haven, twins. I was told my kids are here, I don't know what room Jayne's in," I explain, trying to stay calm. "Are they alright? I mean, why were my babies transferred out of her room?"

"I'll just go in and get one of the nurses for you," he replies, but doesn't stop me when I follow behind after he swipes his keycard at the door.

I signal Tin to stay back. Once in the room, the guy in scrubs approaches the nurses' station and I head toward the only cradle holding two babies. Sure enough, the name card reads, King.

"There you are, sweet babies," I whisper to them as I reach out to touch my daughter's tiny foot.

"What do you think you're doing?" Comes a stern voice behind me and I turn my head to glare at the nurse, my hand frozen mid-air. "Wash your hands before you touch them!"

"Oh, yeah," I gulp, properly chastised. I suppose that *is* one of the basic things that I should have known. There's a sink just behind their crib, actually several sinks are spaced out around the room, so I quickly complete that task. "I got excited, sorry. I don't need a gown or gloves though, do I? Are they healthy?"

She lets out a deep exhale and a smile replaces the stern expression from a moment ago.

"Thomas and Josephine are the healthiest babies in this room. I'm going to assume you're Mr. King?"

I nod to confirm my identity, but my throat tightens up, making it too hard to speak. Jayne fucking named the kids without asking me? I can't have this nurse thinking I'm some deadbeat dad, so I continue to nod before reaching down, sliding one of my callused fingers along my little girl's face.

"Josephine's a mouthful for a little one, so we'll just be calling her Joey," I say when I can finally speak. "I need to know why they're in here, I was away on business and just got back. I was expecting to see Jayne in a room with them. I have her on my insurance, so that shouldn't be an issue."

"I'll have the doctor speak to you, but your, um, well, their mother became agitated when she couldn't breastfeed them and I went to fetch a specialist to work with her. I wasn't gone more than twenty minutes, but she walked out of the hospital before I got back. There was a note saying you would be by for them and she would see you at home," the nurse says, reaching into her pocket and coming back up with a scrap of paper in her hand. "I apologize for telling you like this, but we will need to make sure they'll be safe and cared for when they're released."

I ignore the paper she's holding out to me; my

stomach is churning up a storm and nothing will ever be right between Jayne and me if I look at it. "Is it that post-partum thing?"

"Depression. I'm not qualified to say, but the doctor will sit down with you," she says, looking over her shoulder as though worried she's saying too much. "And her, when she's ready."

"My children will be well cared for; I swear on my life they will be," I vow, putting my hand over my son's stomach and grinning in surprise when I feel his belly rumble. At least until the smell hits me. "Oh God!"

"Daddy duty starts now," she says, covering her nose and her smile at my reaction with her hand. "You may want to grab a pair of those gloves, this will probably be messy. I'm Elena, by the way."

"Parker," I grunt.

While I had intended on watching Elena show me what to do, she deftly put Thomas in my arms and nudged me toward a changing table. After what seemed like a half pound of wipes, the little bugger was cleaned up and I was thinking that Joey might be my favorite. Until the smell from her diaper hit me when I was putting him down next to her. Son of a...

"I believe you know what to do now, I'll just get the doctor," Elena says and my mouth drops open. Thankfully, she points me out to one of the other nurses who keeps a close eye on me while I clean up after my little princess.

And officially decide that I don't have a favorite child after all. Smelly little fuckers, both of them.

I look up to see Tin with a shit-eating grin aimed at me through the window and remember what I said when he delivered the news yesterday.

'*Fucking twins, man.*' I mouth the words to him and he throws his head back with laughter.

I stayed with my babies that night while Tin went home and loaded the car seats into my old Bronco, gathering things from the list Elena gave him so I could take them home the next morning.

That was the first of many mornings that I was the only one around to take care of Joey and Tommy.

ONE

Me'ansome – *Now*

"Dad! Please!" The desperation in Joey's voice hits me, but of all the fucking things for her to ask me to do.

Tin lets out a chuckle from across the table, apparently hearing her voice loud and clear through the phone, and even he knows I'm going to cave.

"Baby girl, are you sure there's not another way?"

"Not really," she answers in a calmer voice. "I pre-ordered books with four authors and I really wanted pictures. Besides, it could be fun. Maybe Ransom will meet someone."

My glare softens as it shifts from Tin to my son and my mouth draws into a hard line as I try not to grin at the thought. Ransom has zero problems getting laid, but taking him to an author event called Motorcycles, Mobsters, and Mayhem? He'll probably, accidently, make me a grandfather before Joey does.

I'm so grateful to have my daughter back in my life, I can't think of anything I'd deny her. Thankfully, despite being raised by her mother's family, she's truly a good person and I've been tripping over myself to be a bigger part of her life.

While it still grates on me that Axel scooped her up the moment he could—and before she found me—I have to admit that he makes her happy and treats her the way every father would want for their daughter. Of course, she has him wrapped as tightly around her little finger as she has the three of us.

Not that Axel doesn't get grumpy about having acquired a father and brother-in-law that want to spend as much time as possible with his wife. Nearly five days back, when Axel was on a work trip, Joey convinced her brother to go for a hike with her on some trail she'd heard about. Smack dab in the middle of their bonding time, doesn't she miss a step and twist her leg all up? They were nearly five miles from her truck with no cell reception.

To say Axel thought the worst when he got home that afternoon and couldn't find his wife is the understatement of the year. At his call, me and some of my men hit the road and were halfway down to

Flagstaff when the twins got ahold of me to let me know what was going on. I sent most of the guys back, but I knew that Tin was coming with me no matter what I said.

We pulled up to the hospital to find Ransom in the parking lot, sitting in his sister's truck with a black eye. Tin stayed with him while I went inside to find Axel getting scolded by an orderly. The poor guy was trying to wheel Joey out of the hospital, as per regulations, but Axel scooped her out of the chair and was determined to carry her.

"It's just a sprained ankle, Dad," she called out when she saw me.

"And a torn meniscus. She may need surgery," Axel growled.

"My knee doesn't hurt that much. Dad, why don't you all stay with us..."

"Not Ransom," Axel growled again. "They gave her a pain killer. It hurt her plenty."

"Axel, it wasn't his fault. I wasn't paying attention," Joey had insisted, rubbing a hand along his jawline in an attempt to soothe him. "I'm alright."

By then, we were outside and Joey gasped when she saw her brother's face. "Axel!"

"I'm alright too," Ransom said, jumping back into goading his large brother-in-law.

Axel just let out a sigh, knowing he was in for it.

"Parker, you can stay with us. Tin and Ransom can get rooms at the clubhouse."

"Plan on breakfast at our house tomorrow," Joey had called to them, giving Axel a look that just dared him to argue. He sighed again and nodded.

After that, I decided it was best to bring my son with us on our 'business' trip, rather than leaving him in close proximity to Axel. Originally, Joey and Axel were going to ride part of the way with us, but with her on crutches that got cancelled.

"Text me the information," I say, conceding to my daughter. "With details on what I'm picking up."

"Oh, and can you take pictures with some of the authors? I've gotten to be friendly with some of them and am so bummed I can't meet them."

"Pictures?" I just want to confirm that I heard her right as I pinch the top of my nose.

"Yes, Dad. I love you and really appreciate this," she adds, making me sit up straight again as we end the call.

"So, we're going back through Houston?" Tin confirms, cocking an eyebrow at me, highlighting the vein that occasionally bulges across his forehead and back along his shaved head.

"Houston?" Ransom asks, barely looking up from the food he's scoffing down.

"There's some kind of book thing going on," I

explain to him. "She needs us to pick up some books she bought and meet some friends she made."

"Oh, the smut she loves to read?" my son asks, shaking his head.

"Please, Tommy-boy," Tin snorts out, laughing. "Say that to her face."

"Yeah, there's an author event, romance authors and readers go to meet each other and talk, I don't know—about books and sex, I guess," I tell my son.

Tin and Ransom share a look before they start laughing in earnest.

"I don't know why you're laughing so hard," I tell them. "You're coming with me."

Suddenly, I'm the only one chuckling.

Piper

"Dammit, Paige! Where are you?" I nearly scream into her voicemail for what feels like the dozenth time. "I don't know what to do and can't believe you're flaking on me like this."

I review my list of pre-orders and almost cringe on how much I've already spent without walking into the room, but I refuse to feel guilty over buying books. The seating chart was in the reader group, so I've planned out my path already. I'm going to run back and see Kristine Allen and Kristine Duggar to get my first load of books to stow away at Paige's table before I meander through the rest of the room.

Really, I'm just killing time, trying to ignore the sick feeling in my stomach when a text message pops up.

Paige: *Sorry, I couldn't find my phone the past couple of days. Look, I got stuck in Nevada and need you to fill in for me today. If I'm not there, I won't get accepted to other signings. Huge favor, but you know the books as well as I do. Just tell them that your credit card reader isn't working, keep whatever cash you make, and I have my QR code printed up to accept payments that way also.*

Nevada! What on Earth is she doing there? That means Paige had no intention of making the signing since she went in the complete opposite direction from where we are currently living.

Me: *No! No! No! You can't be doing this to me!!!*

Paige: *Don't forget you love me! They'll never know the difference.*

Me: *Did those vipers put you up to something? What is going on?*

Paige: *I'm good, I just have to deal with something.*

Fuck. Paige is *not* good if she feels the need to tell me she's good. Our family is behind her absence, I just know it. And as much as I want to call them and chew them out, all that will do is hand them my cell phone number.

This is the sucky part of being an identical twin. It was fun to stand in for her when we were kids, but not in our mid-twenties.

Granted, she's covered for me a time or two also; like that miserable semester that Mom made me join theater so I would 'come out of my shell'. I like my shell. I'm very comfortable in it.

I should have prepared myself for this the moment Paige asked me to bring her bags, that she was just going to get on the road a few hours later than planned. We were always going to drive separately, so it didn't seem like a big deal, but nope, ever the optimist I took her at her word.

I've been looking forward to this signing for nearly a year, even though Paige said she could get me in as her assistant, I bought my VIP ticket so I could get all the goodies and not feel like I have to be on hand to help her out every minute.

Paige and I share a Kindle and there are so many authors that I've read for years who'll be here today. Two years ago, when Paige said she was going to start writing, I just smiled and nodded, thinking that, like everything else, she'd lose interest in it after a few months.

But she's actually really good and in helping her

out with her social media presence, I found out about book signings and this was going to be our first one. The pride I felt at thinking of my sister sitting among these authors is slowly and steadily turning into mind-numbing terror.

I've got this. I've totally got this. I repeat to myself for the hundredth time as I wheel Paige's bags into the event room.

God, what was I thinking? No, dammit, I've got this. Tapping down on my fear, I continue to convince myself that I can talk about her books reasonably well. It's not like it's a job interview.

Fuck! No. Don't think about job interviews!

Total kryptonite.

Okay, seriously, I can do this.

Looking around the room as authors start setting up their tables there's a lot of joking and cama-raderie and I feel like such a fraud. This should be Paige's moment to shine.

Me: *Are you sure I can't just say you couldn't be here?*

Paige: *No. Be me. You know me better than anyone.*

Sighing, I shake my head and wonder why it feels like she needs an alibi for something. I love my sister dearly, but I am not going to jail for her.

I would not do well in jail.

Opening the bags she packed, I take out the metal shelving unit and start lining up her books. She has eight titles out so far, six of which meet the 'motorcycle' criteria for this signing: Motorcycles, Mobsters, and Mayhem.

Across the aisle from me, a family comes in with crates of items and I hear someone shout, "Teagan!", quickly getting the small blonde woman's attention.

Holy shit! That's gotta be Teagan Brooks. I wish I had time to fangirl because her Blackwings series is amazing, but I have to focus on setting up the table and silently pray that Paige will materialize.

Hmm, maybe I could write some science fiction romance. Dammit, Piper, focus on setting up this fiasco.

Looking back at the space left on the table after the books are on it, I start playing with the best way to layout the swag. Paige readily handed over the reins when we discussed the giveaways, and I *may* have gone a bit overboard with everything I bought, but I had a lot of fun hunting down items that were unique.

"Hey! Are you Paige Kyle?" comes a raspy voice from the table behind mine. I tentatively smile at the friendly looking woman and nod. "I'm Darlene, I read a couple of your books, and want to buy some before we pack it in later, alright?

"Oh my God! Really?" Holy shit. That's got to be Darlene Tallman and I had pre-ordered a book from her also.

"You best hold a set for me too," the woman at the table adjoining Darlene's says and I instantly know that she has to be Liberty Parker as the two of them frequently co-write. "I got her reading your books, so I get first dibs."

I nod dumbly and fumble my response. "Um, my sister, Piper, pre-ordered something from you and asked that I grab it since she can't make it now. When you get a chance, can I get it from you? We love all of your books, and I can't believe you've read mine! I barely know what I'm doing."

"You need any help, you let us know. Who are you here with?" Darlene asks and when I indicate that I'm flying solo her eyes widen. "You need a bathroom break or anything, you just tap one of us on the shoulder and one of us or our assistant will help you out."

Someone comes up to talk to her before I can even respond, but suddenly, that feeling of impending doom has disappeared and I know that today is going to be fun. Once my table is set up, I run back upstairs to my room to shower and change out of my sweats.

I barely make it downstairs before the doors open and, sadly, missed the group photo. Walking past the line of people waiting to go in makes me wish I was with them, but I push my nerves aside and hang onto the positive vibes I was feeling earlier.

Right until I walk into a wall.

"What the hell?" a deep voice growls out.

Oh, God, it wasn't a wall, is the first thought in my addled mind when I look up at the large man in the cut. When he squints his eyes, the array of wrinkles seem to highlight their bright green color and I think he's speaking, but I'm still trying to catch my breath.

"What?" I ask as he looks at me expectantly, his face softening as I stare up at him in a near daze.

"What's your name, beautiful?"

"Piper. Um, Paige," I spit out, now focused on his lips.

"You a writer, Piper-Paige?" he asks, smirking at my obvious slip.

"No. Yes." I tell my second set of truth and lies, suddenly realizing that today will be a disaster.

"Christ, woman," he growls again, getting frustrated with my answers as he runs his large hand through his hair. "Are you on this fucking list?"

He holds up his phone to show me a list of authors that nearly mirrors the ones that I had pre-ordered from.

"No. But you can't miss Sapphire, this is her show. Kristine Allen, MariaLisa, Verlene, oh, Desiree Lafawn and Melissa Filla… This list is like my Holy Grail." I nearly moan, looking to either side of him for the woman who I want to be friends with; surprised when I only see a younger carbon copy of him, standing just beyond him. "Um, are those *your* favorite authors?"

The guy I've pegged to be his son snickers and I instantly narrow my eyes at him, until the older man draws my attention back to his mesmerizing green eyes. The humor and warmth reflected there have me leaning toward him and I deeply inhale, instantly wondering how anyone could smell so good without a product from a bottle.

"My daughter couldn't make it. Is there a fucking map or something—so I can get in and out as fast as possible?" he asks me, his deep voice sending a shiver down my spine.

I shrug, feeling like a fraud once again. "There might be, I know they showed the seating chart in the reader group, but I'm guessing that won't help you too much. I'm down the second aisle and I saw some of the banners for a couple of those authors in the row behind me. I know Darlene and Liberty are over there for sure."

Oh, God, I'm talking too much, I think to myself as his eyes seem to glaze over. Shut it, Piper. I squeeze my eyes shut, but he's still there, smiling down at me when I open them.

"Doors are about to open, we need all authors inside now," a voice calls and I turn, darting away from him without another word, as if my life depends on making it to my table before the readers are let in.

Once there, I long, not only to be a reader, but to spend a few more minutes with a man that I'm inexplicably drawn to. I dated here and there in college, but it was more out of curiosity than feeling an intense attraction to the men I'd go out with. Ugh, compared to that guy, calling them *men* is like comparing a clementine to a grapefruit.

Paige was always with someone, from our high school years until about a year ago— even if it only lasted a couple of weeks. I envied how she seemed to hum with excitement at the start of each new relationship, but I have never felt that before.

Until now. And who does it happen with? An actual, honest to goodness biker with the looks to rival most Hollywood actors. Oh, God, with a son who didn't look that much younger than me.

I start chuckling to myself. That guy thought he was going to get in and out?

Every woman in the room is going to try to stop him, and the guy I'm guessing is his son, for pictures.

TWO

Me'ansome – *Now*

I dragged my son here early enough, claiming the tickets that Joey had bought for her and Axel, but the fucking crowd waiting to get in is more than I expected. Ransom is too hungover to care what's going on, but then someone literally walks into me.

Not being a small guy, I can honestly say that has never happened to me before.

I'm close to losing my shit when I turn around, but how can I when this woman, barely older than my daughter looks up at me with doe eyes and lets out a sigh?

Then she lies to me, not once, but twice in quick succession. The questions weren't even the life-or-death type, so I find myself even more intrigued. She barely spares a glance at my son, but it's when she leans closer to me that I feel my cock harden in my jeans.

Damn, it feels good to know I still have *it* at my age.

Before I know it, she goes running off.

"Go back to that table and get a map or list of authors. There has to be an organized way to navigate this," I growl at Ransom before going to stand next to the door that the woman just ran through.

"There's a line," another lady tells me, looking thoroughly annoyed with me not giving a fuck about the hundred or so people that are plainly standing in said line.

Grinning at her, I'm suddenly inspired when the banner just behind her catches my eye. "My son's a model, we've got to just sneak in as soon as he gets here."

There's a collective gasp from the women waiting, with one poking her head out from the crowd to add, "You should model, also."

"Yeah, oh, is that your son?" the original woman asks me just as I feel him at my back.

"Here's the map thing," Ransom says, looking confused when she hands him a blank canvas and a marker. "What am I supposed to do with that?"

"Sign it, then follow me," I growl at him, elbowing him as I grab the map from him.

"Um, excuse me," another lady with a badge that reads 'Volunteer' sidles up to us. "Do you have your name badges? Who are you with?"

"A couple of authors, darling," I mumble before yanking open the door and pulling my son through it.

"What the fuck was that?" Ransom asks while trying to keep up with me. I figured I'd head for the furthest corner of the room and hope that volunteer doesn't get too curious.

"We're getting in and out, and I'm sure as fuck not standing in that line," I answer him, looking over my shoulder to make sure security hasn't been called. God knows how I'd explain that to Joey. "I told them you were a model, so play along if anyone else asks for an autograph."

"Huh!" Ransom stops in his tracks and points at a banner a couple of tables in from the aisle. "He kinda looks like you. What's up with having a senior citizen on a cover?"

"I'm not a..." my voice trails off when I see his grin and know that I fell into that trap way to easy.

Before I know, it Ransom cuts over to get a closer look at the banner, and I follow him, smiling and nodding at the different women sitting at their tables. Just beyond where Ransom is taking pictures of a banner—with a model that looks nothing like me—I see the cute little liar who ran into me earlier.

"Hey, Dad," Tommy says, looking up from his conversation with an author whose table is covered with books. Nearly more than I've read in my lifetime, and I'm completely impressed by the fact that she's written so many books. "She said Joey preordered from her, get over by her banner for a picture."

"Come on! I won't bite," she laughs, throwing me a wink.

Oh, fuck. I'm pretty sure she does.

My son snaps the picture and while he's sending it to Joey, I see the volunteer walking down the main aisle.

"Ransom, grab the books," I order him before turning to cut through to the space occupied by the author behind Darlene.

The woman, whom I'm guessing is Piper and not Paige looks up at me with her large, expressive eyes and narrows her brows at me.

Ignoring the fact that I invaded her private space, I walk to the front of her table and look over her books. It's not easy, but I keep a straight face when I see all of the guys on the covers of her biker series.

"My daughter couldn't make it, so she asked that

I pick up her pre-orders for her," I repeat what I had originally told her, a little rattled that she's only watching me and not saying anything.

"No judgement," she says as the corner of her mouth curls up. "Whatever you like to read is fine with me."

"Have you decided what your name is yet?" I ask trying to put her on the defensive since I'm not used to a woman talking to me like that.

She points to the banner behind her, one that reads Paige Kyle in large letters across the top.

"Which one of these would you recommend for my daughter?" I ask her next, indicating her titles.

"Maybe this one," she says, barely missing a beat.

My eyes follow her finger to a book that is displayed separately from the others and I frown at the cover. There's a half-naked man and a wolf—what the fuck is this nonsense?

When I look back at her, she does her damnedest not to smile. "What's that about?"

"Shapeshifters," she answers, cocking her head to the side. "You know? People that can turn into animals."

"Like a werewolf? And it's romance?" I ask, trying to wrap my head around this concept. "You're totally fucking with me."

"Well, I can't imagine your daughter needs too

many more books on bikers," she responds, finally letting her smile break free as she eyes my cut. "That's really brave, y'know?"

"What is?" I find myself returning her smile, without really knowing why.

"Wearing your cut and walking around most of these women. Did any of the photographers stop you yet?"

When I shake my head, she laughs to herself.

"So, it's fifteen if you want the book. Free gift with purchase and cash is preferred," are the next words out of her slightly chapped, red lips and I find myself reaching for my wallet.

"Keep the gift and have dinner with me tonight instead," I tell her, enjoying seeing her eyes widen in surprise before they lock on someone standing beside me.

"Move over, hot stuff," an older woman crows at me, taking her time as she looks me up and down. "Paige, if you don't go out with him, I will! And I'm Cielli, I pre-ordered some books from you. I know you're really private about posting photos of yourself, so I want one, but won't post it online, deal? Here, take our picture, Hottie McTottie, unless you'd like to join us?"

"Yeah, Dad, why don't you pose with them?" My

soon-to-be murdered son pipes up, as he helpfully reaches for the woman's cellphone.

Next thing I know I'm standing between Piper and a woman who's probably a few years older than me, with bright pink hair.

"Give me your number." My arm is still around the younger woman; even as she hands over a bag full of books to Cielli. She looks slightly dazed as she's entering the numbers into my mobile and I quickly hit the send button to make sure the phone on the table lights up, once it does I lean down to her ear. "I'll meet you in the lobby at 6:30."

"I never agreed to have... Wait! The book you bought," she squeaks out, completely flustered. "Who do I make it out to?"

"Joey," I answer her and wait as she signs it, smirking when she only writes a large 'P' instead of a full name.

"Thank you." She smiles up at me when she hands the book over.

"Don't make me wait, Piper," I whisper, enjoying the guilty expression on her face. "Who the fuck is Paige?"

"My sister, she needed me to cover for her," she whispers back before turning away. "Now I've got to work!"

"She's hot," Ransom announces when we're walking away from her table.

"And *mine*. Why don't you go see about finding us a couple rooms for tonight? And let Tin know we'll stay in the area," I tell him, breaking away when I see a banner listing one of the authors Joey bought books from.

I pull up to the hotel where the signing took place, ten minutes early and am surprised to see Piper standing well outside of the doors, looking nervous.

"Sweetheart," I start, with a warning my voice.

"I know what you said, but the after-party is about to start and if they spot us, they'll drag us in," she blurts out, and I admit, she has a point.

"Did you want to go to that?" I ask her point blank, wondering what it is about this woman that would make me consider walking into the lion's den if she wanted to go.

"I wanted to, when I was coming as a reader," she answers honestly. "Look, can we get out of here and we'll talk?"

"You're wearing a skirt," I say, pointing out the obvious. Not that she doesn't look amazing, but between that and her sandals, my bike isn't the best mode of transportation anymore.

"I'm parked right there," she immediately replies, pointing at a blue Silverado.

Nodding, I go to park my bike without a word, but make it back to the truck before she gets into the driver's seat.

"I'm driving." I slip the keys out of her hand and start to escort her around the cab when she leans up on her tip toes in what I think is an attempt to kiss me.

"Not a goddamn chance," she whispers barely brushing her lips across my ear-lobe and pulling back from me as she jingles the keys she had swiped back when I was distracted.

Reaching behind her neck, I decide that the price of me riding passenger is worth more than her chaste kiss and lean down to her, parting her lips with my tongue I wind mine around hers, and pretending for a quick moment, that I have the upper hand.

With a moan, she finally wraps her arms around my shoulders and the feel of the cool metal keys at my neck sends chills down my spine.

"Ya got a second, Prez?" Tin's voice comes from behind me and I whip my head around, my eyes shooting daggers at him. I think he would have laughed, but his eyes drift to the woman in my arms and he lets out a low whistle instead. "Fuck. Sorry, but I need a word."

Reaching behind Piper, I open the door and help her inside her truck.

"What's wrong?" I ask him, not missing that his eyes remain focused on Piper.

"Nothing in particular," he says, shrugging and I know how he gets when he's away from home too long. "Just thought I'd ride through the night and make sure everything's square back at the clubhouse. I packed up about a dozen of Joey's books, so you and Ransom can split up the rest of them."

"Are you good to ride?" I'm always surprised at how thoughtful he is when it comes to my kids, and know that Joey will be happy to have, at least some of, her books tomorrow since she's probably pulling her hair out by now.

"Yeah, I slept this afternoon and I'll stop along the way," he nods. "Ransom has a couple girls back in the room and I'm not feeling it."

"Check in every six hours," I tell him, grinning when he tells me to enjoy myself.

I sure as fuck hope I get the chance to.

Piper

After establishing that I'm happy going to a Tex-Mex restaurant, he guides me to a place he had apparently scoped out earlier. Turning off the truck, I'm startled when I feel his rough hand on my wrist. Looking down at his hand, rather than his face, he simply points to where my left hand is on the door handle before waving his hand horizontally.

Hmmm, apparently chivalry isn't dead. It's just about twenty years older than me.

My heart feels like it's thrumming out of my chest as I wait for him to circle the vehicle and open the door, taking my hand to help me out.

"What is it with little girls and big-ass trucks?" he asks, unable to keep the laughter out of his voice.

"I am perfectly average height, thank you," I answer back, narrowing my eyebrows at him. "And who are you comparing me to with that statement?"

"My daughter," he laughs, running a finger along the crease between my brows. "She's maybe got an inch or two on you and also needs the running board to get into her truck."

"Oh," I sigh out the word, remembering her list of authors that she had pre-ordered from, and ask the next logical question as we walk into the restaurant. "Why wasn't she here?"

"Joey and Ransom—my son who was there earlier —went hiking a few days back and she sprained her ankle and tore her meniscus." I nearly shudder at the thought of being laid up like that and not being able to get on the road. "I'm a sucker for anything she asks me for. So, she's back home with her husband and I get to have dinner with you."

"I don't know how to respond to that. When you showed me her preorder list earlier, I saw a kindred soul I would have loved to talk about books with, but it's probable I wouldn't have just had the best kiss of my life if she was here." On the drive over, I decided to throw caution to the wind and let him know what I'm thinking.

Unlike the actual Paige Kyle, I have always approached life cautiously and don't do casual relationships, but after running through the gauntlet, doing my best to act like Paige today, I decided to gift myself with going the distance with Me'ansome; that brings up my next question.

"What does Me'ansome mean? And am I pronouncing it right?" As we're being seated and give our drink order, I ask about the name on his cut, feeling foolish about being on a date with someone when I don't know their actual name.

"It's a Cornish term of endearment, usually for a mother to her son. My given name is Parker, so take your pick," he says. "Now, why don't you tell me why you were imitating your sister today?"

"Oh, no, we're still on the topic of you!" I inform him, my eyes widening when a fishbowl sized margherita is placed in front of me.

"Mind if I grab those keys?" he asks, shifting his gaze between the bottle of beer he has and my drink.

Handing them over, I ask about his 'road name' again.

"To be honest, most of the guys call me 'Mean-some', and I don't blame them 'cause I know they feel like they're calling me handsome. I was in a unique position, where I dictated my road name, so fuck 'em."

"That's how Paige lives her life," I quietly respond to his sentiment while I catalog the fact that the large man across the table from me is a momma's boy at heart. "She just doesn't give a fuck about what anyone thinks or what the ramifications of her actions are. We didn't really have a typical upbringing, no idea who our dad is, but our mom's family, well, I guess the nicest term is that they're grifters. I just could never stand to look someone in the eye and lie to them."

"That's probably for the best, because you're awful at it," he says, reaching across the table to cup my left hand within both of his.

"I really am," I say, laughing before I direct the straw to my mouth for another big gulp of my drink. "Mom used to try to force me into acting classes, Paige would go for me—oh, we're identical twins, I don't know if I mentioned that."

He leans back against his side of the booth and laughs when I say that, I just cock my head to the side, lifting an eyebrow to get an explanation has him lifting his beer for a swig.

"My brother and I were identical twins. My children, Joey and Ransom are fraternal, of course, being different sexes."

"Oh my God!" I squeal, happy to have common ground that we can exchange stories about. "What was the worst thing you ever got in trouble for that he did and not you?"

"Murder or human trafficking." His eyes hold mine, stopping me dead in my tracks.

"Well, that sucks," I breathe out, once I am able to pick my jaw up from the ground.

"Yeah, and too heavy a topic for tonight," he says as the food comes and we enjoy the first few bites in silence.

"How old are Joey and Ransom?" I ask and instantly feel my cheeks turning pink under his knowing stare.

"They're twenty-one," he answers, drawing his

brows together like he thought of something unpleasant.

"And their mother?"

"Other than to tell you we haven't been together in over twenty years, it's my turn now." This answer gives me a hint about what caused his frown. "What's your sister up to that she didn't show for this?"

"I honestly don't know," I tell him. "We inherited our great-aunt's home a few years back, so we only have the property tax to pay on it. I'm a consultant and can work from anywhere and after a long stretch of jobs she took as cover while working on cons with our family, she started writing and it really took off. I'm really proud of what she's creating and I think it's giving her the confidence to break ties with our mother and her family."

"A consultant, I've always wanted to ask what the fuck that means exactly," he says, reaching across the table to wipe something from the corner of my mouth with his thumb, leaving a trail of tingles in its wake.

"Well, I tell fairly successful business owners how to become more successful," I answer that with a relieved grin, pleased his question focused on me and not the hot-fucking-mess of the family that spawned us.

"And this is based on your years of experience as a successful business owner?" he counters, calling me out on the bullshit that is my career path.

"No. It is based on algorithms, on tried and true methods mixed with current trends."

"How old are you?"

"Twenty-four," I answer, hoping that he'll share his age this time.

"I'm forty-three. Where does that leave us?" Me'ansome leans forward, reaching out to take one of my hands in his.

"Wh-what do you mean?" I stutter out, trying to buy myself a moment as my heart rate shoots through the roof.

"I mean, what are your thoughts on fucking a man old enough to be your father?" His eyes have narrowed as he watches my face intently even as he lifts his beer up for a swig.

"Oh, my God, what if you are my father?" I ask, leaning forward with wide eyes, just to fuck with him.

It works, kind of, as he starts choking on his drink.

"Bite your fucking tongue," he rasps out, letting me know I won't have to give him the Heimlich maneuver.

"I'm kidding, odds are that my dad was a

neighbor who died before we were born," I say, trying to reassure him. Although I shudder at the thought that it was probably my grandfather who killed the man. "I don't have any daddy issues, but I would like to explore this."

"You're much better at being honest than lying," he says with a wink, pulling his hand back across the table.

"Thank you," I say, shifting my hand to toss my hair over my shoulder—once again forgetting that I had it chopped off last week.

"Where do you live?" he asks suddenly.

"Right now, we live in the Oklahoma panhandle, but I'm going on the road for a few weeks to scope out some other areas."

"Are you from there?"

"No. We have been fixing up our great-aunt's house. Paige and I are both fairly secure financially right now, so we'll sell it and land where we land. How about you?"

"I'm from Cornwall, but I've lived in Southern Utah for most of my life," he says and before I can ask him for more details, he leans across the table to declare his intentions. "I want you for dessert, Piper. I don't want to be here another minute longer, I'm old, I don't date, and I've been trying really hard to be good to you. Now, I want to get you back to your room to show you I'm much more than the best kiss you've ever had."

"Oh. Okay, then." I nod, leaning over I take a long, deep sip of my drink and by the time I've opened my eyes again, he's thrown a bunch of twenties on the table and is standing up, waiting by my side with his hand outstretched to help me up.

His arm easily slides around me as we walk out to my truck and we hold hands across the center seat of the truck, like it's the most natural thing in the world. We're nearly back to the resort when I put a name to what is happening.

I feel safe.

Since he pulled up on his motorcycle, I haven't looked over my shoulder one time. I didn't enter an unknown restaurant and immediately scan it for someone who looked out of place.

I've had butterflies in my stomach, not the feeling of a heavy weight on my shoulders, and not once have I used the rear view mirrors to check for someone who might be following me. Waiting to corner me alone and remind me that I'm not really free. That my family expects what they think they're owed—simply because I was born into it.

THREE

Me'ansome - *Then*

I turn on the light next to my chair when Jayne
stumbles through the door, her keys falling to
the floor rather than the table she was aiming for.

"Thomas still isn't asleep?" she slurs out, barely
looking at the baby I'm feeding.

"This is Joey," I answer, trying to keep my voice
neutral as she kicks off her heals and heads into the
kitchen.

Returning with two bottles of beer, she puts one
down next to me and takes a swig of hers before
briefly sweeping her eyes over our daughter.

"Here, I can put Josephine to bed. She can finish
her bottle there tonight," she says, stressing Joey's

full name since she insists that nicknames are *common,* and reaches for our little girl.

"Why don't you go to bed," I answer, holding my child closer to my chest without disturbing her bottle. I look down to see Joey's eyes are closed even as she threads her fingers through my beard. I meant to shave it today since Tommy loves to give it a yank when I least expect it, but the sitter didn't show up and I was too fucking swamped to handle that.

"Oh! Is Daddy mad at me? Why don't you turn me over your knee and spank me? Like you used to, if you can remember that far back, *Old Man?*" she sneers at me and tilts her beer back for a big swig.

"I think I'll pass." I tilt my chin in the direction of the light, flaky substance that easily shows on her evenly tanned thighs. She's obviously already been fucked tonight and I don't like playing second fiddle to anyone. "There's no doubt in my mind that Joey and Tommy are mine, but if you turn up pregnant again, you best hit the road."

"I have post-partum depression," Jayne says, pulling herself up to her full height. "You talk to me like that when I'm suffering like this? You aren't a man at all, are you? This is why I need to go find tenderness from someone else."

I heavily exhale, not even caring enough about her to fight anymore. Tenderness, huh? I bite down on the smile that threatens to turn this into a full blown scream-fest. Jayne always liked it rough.

The first few months after the twins were born, she flooded the house with tears, but I could live with that. At least until I realized it wasn't the therapist she was going to see every other day. The running around started before the twins hit six months and now, just past their first birthday, I just want her gone.

But if there's any hope of some peace the rest of the night, kicking her out will have to wait until she sleeps off whatever she's on.

I stand to get Joey back to bed and leave Jayne standing there; refusing to give her the fight she wants. Joey fusses when I put her down, no doubt upset from my confrontation with her mom. The past months have proven to me that children can sense tension, even though they're too young to understand our words.

Leaning over the side of her crib, I stroke her head, happy to have a reason to avoid Jayne in the other room. I check that Tommy is alright before I pull down the Murphy bed, one that occupied this room long before I met Jayne, and crawl into my sleeping bag.

Tonight, I'm just happy that the divorce lawyer dropped off the paperwork earlier. Tomorrow, I'll work on getting Jayne to sign the twins' custody over to me.

"He wants to meet with you," Tin insists.

The timing sucks, but I've been putting it off too long and we need to keep our Mexican contacts happy if we're going to keep giving us priority over some of their bigger clients.

That and I'll have to figure out who I can trust to watch my kids. Jayne's been gone nearly two months, and while she hen-scratched some shit out on the custody documents I presented her with, I doubt it'll stand up in a court of law.

With a bit of luck, I can handle the round-trip to the Mexican border and meeting in less than a day. Considering Tin will be with me, there's not a lot of choices for twin-duty.

That time my enforcer's Ol' Lady stepped up to watch my kids, but it was the next time I was forced to find a sitter, at the last minute, that I lost half of what I held dear in this world.

Tommy was always a little smaller and fussier than his sister, and if she got a runny nose, he got a full-fledged cold. It was earlier in the afternoon when the teenager watching them, called to tell me that he woke up feverish. By the time I had made it home, both he and the sitter had started projectile vomiting.

I went into full panic mode.

Tin was on his way back from a run, and I couldn't reach my enforcer, Brick, to get his wife over to my place. The only one I could reach was my brother's regular girl, Polly. She came over once I promised her a few hundred to care for Joey while I dropped off the high school kid and took Tommy to the hospital.

Hearing the news when he returned to the clubhouse, Tin rode to the hospital to get an update, just in time for Tommy's release. When we got back to my house, he was right behind me and saw that something was wrong before I did—revving his motor to signal me.

My stomach immediately clenched up when, beyond the screen door, I could tell that the front door was wide open—the air-conditioning seeping out to warm the Arizona summer.

"Stay here," I screamed over the roar of Tin's bike, pointing to the back seat of my SUV.

He quickly shuts down his ride and looked over at Tommy after settling into the driver's seat.

When I enter, Polly is half on, half off the sofa and I see an empty bottle of champagne, that's way out of her price range, sitting on the side table.

Racing past her, a part of my soul slowly seeps away as I search each room for my baby girl. My little Joey, but she isn't fucking here.

Polly should have died that day.

If it wasn't for my brother, Parson, showing up with some of his cartel buddies, I probably *would* have murdered her. As it is, she'll never show her face around my MC again.

"Who can we count on as friends?" I asked Tin, after three days of searching for Jayne and Joey.

Unfortunately, my brother and his promise of illegal pussy, drugs, and cash from south of the border have poisoned some of the men that had ridden by my side for years.

"We have several solid guys, but the more men we send, the tighter her family will close ranks. I have an idea, you might not like it, but I need you to trust me." Tin's face is as serious as I've ever seen it, so I exhale and nod.

I had already tracked Jayne's ass back east and I nearly got arrested outside of her family's home. Fucking hell. I had never been so close to a private home the likes of where her family lived.

The grounds were nearly impenetrable, but the closer I got to the actual house, the more certain I was that I'd never find Joey and get out without being arrested. I also knew with absolute certainty, that if I was arrested, I'd never see either of my children again.

Misdirection was my only avenue of escape, so my gloved hand picked up a rock and hurled it through a window, setting off the alarm system. That was my cue to rabbit, and I did, just barely making it over a fence before the security team set eyes on me.

"You want me to call Fetch?" I ask, and I get a smirk from Tin. Fetch is one of two men that I've been friends with longer than him. "He moved to the east coast for a reason, he wanted out of this life."

"Yeah, but he still needs income, right?" Tin throws out. "I say he goes and gets hired on at that fancy fucking house that Jayne moved back to, plus he gets something from you to keep tabs on Joey. Y'know, just until you get her back."

"If he agrees, you'll need to get him fake papers, a full credit history, and set up a regular communication strategy with him," I tell Tin at the same time I pick up the phone to dial one of the few numbers I know by heart.

"He'll agree," Tin's voice is a near whisper.

Fetch picks up on the second ring, but doesn't say a word.

"I need you," I say, not even minding when my voice cracks. "She took my baby girl and I need your help."

"Anytime, anywhere, Me'ansome," without hesitation, Fetch responds, using the name my mother called me more often than she used my given name.

And with those words, he spends the next seventeen years watching over my little girl.

Me'ansome - *Now*

"Wait," Piper says as I pull her truck into a spot close to the main entrance of the resort and my heart drops to my stomach in disappointment. "Can you pull around to the other side of that building? There's a side entrance that's closer to my room and we can bypass the lobby."

Her words throw cold water on the buzz I'd been feeling since we left the restaurant and I just turn to look at her. Not angry, but wishing she felt half of what I have ever since I laid eyes on her.

"I enjoyed dinner," I tell her, trying to be a gentleman. "My bike's right there, so I'll let you go."

"You. Um, you're leaving?" she stutters out and I swear I see her bottom lip tremble a little.

"Look, I get it, there's a major age difference between us and while I want nothing more than to spend the night with you, I'm not going take a pity fuck when you're too embarrassed to be seen with me. Good luck with things," I tell her, reaching for my door as I'm sliding the keys back into her hand.

Her grip surprises me and I look over at her, getting annoyed at her indecision.

"I have no problem being seen with you, Parker." Her voice is huskier than it has been all evening and catches my attention; I frown at her, trying to figure out what her game is. "It's just that if we walk through the lobby or anyone sees us together, people will see you going up to spend the night with Paige. And I don't want that.

"I want you, and I know this is my fault because I went along with Paige's plan, but I don't want to share the idea of you being with her persona. I'm not making any sense, I mean," Piper says, shaking her head in frustration as her eyes bore into me.

That could not have been clearer to me though, so I shift my hand up to cup the back of her head and lean in, meeting her halfway for a kiss. The second our lips connect, I hear her seatbelt release and am more than a little surprised when she climbs across the center to straddle me.

Long moments pass and our kiss slowly moves from desperation to something less frantic, but filled with need just the same, and I know I've never kissed anyone like this before.

"Give me the fucking keys back," I gasp out when our lips part, grinning when she looks confused. "You wanted to park in the other lot, remember?"

"Oh, I, um," she says, looking over her shoulder. Without another sound, her right hand grabs my left forearm, securing her position as she stretches down and across to snag the keys from the passenger floorboard.

"Christ, woman. Are you a gymnast?" Impressed with her moves, I suddenly start praying that she is.

"No, just highly motivated," Piper giggles as she grinds her pelvis down on my hard cock.

"Give me those." I don't give her the chance to respond, I just yank the keys from her and start the truck up, neither one of us giving a fuck that she's dry humping me as I wind the vehicle through the parking lots to get to where she had indicated.

As soon I turn it back off, she's reaching for the door and unentangles herself from me with more grace than I'd be capable of and I reach for her purse before following her, barely remembering to lock her truck up.

I stand there a moment, hoping I can live up to her expectations as I watch her ass sway as she walks up the cobblestone path to the side door and I reach down to adjust myself before I follow her.

We waste no time getting up to her room and I'm barely through the door before she's pulling her top over her head and turning back to me, her arms reaching up to slide my cut off.

"Hold up there a second, sugar. No need to rush," I let her know, placing a finger over her lips. Lifting her, I place her on the desk and Piper does that little movement where it looks like she's trying to brush her hair back, and it finally dawns on me. "Did you just chop your hair off?"

She nods, looking over her shoulder at the mirror behind her, studying her silky, chestnut bob. "I can't get used to it, but I wanted to try something different."

"I think you're hot," I say, standing back and giving her a long appreciative look. She cocks her head to the side before throwing a wink my way and

I reach down to slide her sandals off. "I also suspect you're a little bit of a coward."

"Brave man to call me out like that right now," she sasses back, crossing her arms over her chest, effectively pulling my gaze down to where her tits threaten to pop out of her blue lace bra.

"You knew damn well I'd show up with my bike and you wore that skirt and these shoes," I tell her, holding them up by the straps I just unwound from her ankles.

"I've never been on one before and I was nervous," she confesses what I had already guessed.

"We're going to have to change that," I tell her, wondering why it matters to me. "Slip on out of your skirt now."

She looks shy, but she does what I tell her as I pull the chair up to the desk and start to work on her.

Piper lets out a gasp when she realizes my intention and tries to snap her legs closed, a little too late. I'm already between them and I just grin up at her, letting my finger trail up and down the outside of the panties that match her bra.

They're not an inexpensive set, so it bolsters my confidence that she had similar intentions for how the night was going to go.

I pop my tongue against the roof of my mouth,

shaking my head when she starts to open her pink lips. As soon as she seals them shut again, I slide my hands back along her thighs to grip her ass and pull her to the edge of the desk.

"I meant what I said about wanting dessert." My words are the last ones spoken for quite a while.

With my thumb between her pussy and thigh, I pull the bit of lace to the far side and lean in, opening up her swollen lips with my tongue. From the corner of my eyes, I see Piper's fingers curl around the edge of the desk, and giving her ass a quick squeeze with my other hand and pull it back. Using both thumbs, I slowly explore her with my mouth.

There was a time I ate pussy like it was my vocation, but as the years jaded me that joy became—distasteful, I guess is a good way of saying it. I lick at Piper like I've been in the desert for years and as her breathing hitches more and more, the thought of taking my time seems ridiculous.

Looking up at her, I find her eyes pinned to me as if trying to seal away every detail of this moment in her memory. I shift up just enough to focus on her clit and slide a finger inside her slick, tight tunnel.

Slowly coordinating my movements, I feel her hand, timidly cupping the back of my head and I press down against her harder—silently giving her permission to hold me to her as long and as hard as she needs.

God knows I won't have any reticence about guiding her head on my cock, I think with a grin to myself.

"Please." That single, whispered word comes from her perfect mouth seconds before I feel her orgasm coming on. Her cunt tightens around my finger and her hips buck upward, pushing her slick pussy against my face. "More, Me'ansome."

I pause for a split second, surprised at how different my road name sounds coming from her lips in this moment. She lets out a mewl and holds my head tighter, relaying the importance of where Piper wants me focused in this moment.

As the shudders pass and her body starts to relax, I sweep my tongue down and into her core to taste her sweetness, knowing that I could easily get addicted to her.

"Me'ansome," Piper says in a clearer tone of voice and I look back up at her. "I bought some condoms earlier. I wasn't sure what size, but they're in the drawer next to the bed."

"I have a couple with me," I let her know before I slip the finger that had been inside of her seconds ago, into my mouth to clean it off. Her jaw drops open and as her face flames red, a realization spreads over me and I waste no time confirming it. "Am I the first man to eat you out?"

With her shy nod, I cup her ass again and quickly turn, nearly tossing her on the bed.

"Let's see what size you pegged me for," I say, reaching for the top drawer of the nightstand as she scurries to beat me over there.

"No! Don't," Piper yelps with her ass in the air as she uses both hands to try to hold the drawer closed.

"Christ!" I yell louder than intended when I nearly lose a finger. "How many fucking condoms did you buy?"

"There were so many sizes and I got flustered. I was going to go with *one size fits most*, but I didn't know if that would insult you. Then there's ribbed and Bare Skin and..." She must realize she's babbling because she seems to run out of steam mid-sentence.

"I appreciate your concern for little Parker's feelings." I'm a sarcastic old bastard, what can I say?

"Oh, are they all going to be too big?" Her wide eyes look pitifully down at the selection of condoms.

I grab my heart when she practically growls that zinger at me, but she once again crosses her arms over her chest and all I can focus on is her tits and how badly I want to play with them.

Piper

It's kind of a heady feeling, the way that Parker keeps checking out my boobs. Being a late bloomer, I've always been a little self-conscious about them, but I'm suddenly feeling a lot more confident with my C cups.

"Stop!" The word pops out way louder than I had intended, when he starts to put his knee on the side of the bed to lean down to me. "You have way too many clothes on to climb into this bed."

He shrugs his shoulder, in what I take to be agreement, before he returns to the chair he just vacated. Slowly and methodically, starting with his boots, he pulls off each item—going so far as to neatly line up the contents of his pockets on the desk.

My cheeks flare red at the thought of what he just did to me there, more-so when he just gives me a knowing grin when he turns back to me.

Tonight will go down in my memory for several reasons, but mostly because it was the first time anyone's gone down on me.

And it was completely worth the wait.

That alone has completely surpassed my limited sexual experience altogether, so even if the sex sucks, I won't care. Okay, well, I will because his mouth, and, oh god, his tongue has set the bar really high right now.

He stands up, removing his belt from his jeans before he takes those off, grabbing one of the condoms he had laid on the desk before finally coming back to join me in his boxer-briefs, looking sexy as hell.

"You have a lot of ink," I blurt out, fairly surprised that only one tattoo is placed below where the sleeves of his T-shirt hit his arms.

"And you only have one," he replies, reaching for my arm to kiss the one I have on my wrist. Something Paige and I did on a whim when we turned seventeen.

"I tend to overthink things," I confess one of my traits that my family always saw as a character flaw, but he doesn't look particularly surprised.

"Are you overthinking this? Now?"

"No. I'm—this is right. You made me feel so good, over there," I nervously babble again, my eyes darting to the desk.

"Really? Because I was trying to make you feel good, right here." His wry grin makes another appearance as his finger taps my clit and I tuck my head into the crook of his neck.

Sliding my hand down, I circle the large bulge of his cock over his briefs; rubbing him up and down in a feeble attempt to get to the next stage. I gasp when he quickly unsnaps my bra with one hand before I pull it away.

"You are so fucking gorgeous," he says, pushing me back so he can kiss first one, then the other peak.

Twirling his tongue around each one, and once again taking his time before suckling them. By then, I have my hand inside his shorts and am trying my damnedest to pull him on top of me.

"Is there a time factor I'm unaware of?" Parker growls, his words vibrating around my nipple, sending shivers down my spine.

"I want you," I tell him, need raising my voice an octave higher than it usually sounds.

"I'm a sure thing, honey, but I like to take my time," he replies, resting his chin between my breasts as he looks up at me with his soulful green eyes.

"Maybe you can you take your time the next time?" I ask, giving him a little grin although I already suspect he's not going to give in.

"Patience, Piper," he says, before sliding his briefs down. I let out a sigh when I catch a glimpse of his tumescent cock before I feel it nestle against my pussy.

Without another word, Parker rolls, pulling me to sit on top of him, his large, callused hands grip my hips and pull me snug against his hard-on. "Rub up against me," he directs me and I don't need to be asked twice.

Once I get my rhythm, I look down to see his eyes glued to where his hands had moved up to roll my nipples between his fingers.

I've never understood my sister's confidence, but in this moment a hidden door inside of me cracks open and I feel it as it starts to spread through me. Damn, if this is how she feels all the time, I've been missing out.

There's no subterfuge in Parker's eyes, just his desire for me. I stop moving to lean down and kiss him, needing to feel that connection with him again. His lips move tenderly over mine as our tongues dance together with longing, as the gray and wiry hair on his chest tickles my breasts, his arms wrapping around me to hold me tightly against the hard plains of his body.

"Me'ansome," I say, abruptly ending our kiss, I cup his face with my hands as I use his road name to get his attention. "It's been a really long time for me, and as much as I appreciate all of the patience you're showing, I just really want you to suit up and give me what I need."

He gives a quick nod to his side and I slide off of him, appreciating his body as he rolls the condom on before turning back to me. Our hands reach for each other as if by their own accord and with our fingers intertwined, Parker once again covers me with his body.

His hard cock pressing against my body as he strokes his free hand down my face until he reaches my chin and tilts it up, his eyes searching mine until he softly smiles and kisses me again. Parker subtly shifts, lining his cock up with the entrance to my pussy and I spread my legs wider, bending my knees to give him easier access.

His cock nudges into me, slowly rocking to gain more ground with every forward thrust and while I've never felt more full, I whine around his tongue, wanting to feel all of him.

"Piper?"

"Uh-huh," I moan back.

"Patience."

My eyes fly open with his whispered reminder to find him grinning down at me, leaving no doubt that even though he's now fully inside of me, he will not be rushed.

The next twenty minutes seemed to stretch on for hours as Parker did the one thing I hadn't expected.

He made love to me.

From start to firework-ending finish, he kissed,

nibbled, licked and sucked at my flesh. Any time I would venture a look up to his face, he would be looking at me, watching my reactions to each of his movements until I couldn't stand to look away from him.

And when my muscles started spasming around his length, my hips undulating as he continued to drive his spear into me and I felt like I was drowning, all I could think to do was hold him tighter, certain he'd never let anything happen to me.

I'm not sure how long I floated between sleep and wakefulness, but it was a soft cry coming from my own lips that roused me again when I felt him roll off of me.

"Give me a minute, baby," he said, pressing his lips against my temple and pulling the comforter over my languid body.

I keep my eyes on his back as he stalks to the bathroom and count the seconds until I hear the flush of the toilet and some running water before I see him again. His dick is half-mast, defiantly jutting upwards no matter how hard it had just worked.

My eyes widen when I see he's holding a damp cloth and I blush when he gently swipes it over my pussy, momentarily tensing up until I feel the heat from the warm water he used.

"Do you need anything?" he asks me and I nod,

holding my arms open to him. Usually, these moments post-sex are filled with anxious thoughts or scrambling to get dressed. Since he left no room for doubt that he was planning to stick around for a bit, I simply shake my head at him, waiting for his next move.

Parker leaves the cloth in place and wraps the comforter around both of us as he pulls me into his arms.

I try to think of something to say to him, but the exhaustion from the day overtakes me and it is hours later when I wake up to the sound of him talking on his cell phone.

FOUR

Piper

"Is everything alright?" I ask, looking around as I try to get a sense of what time it is.

"I had missed a couple of calls from Tin," he says, referring to the man I had briefly met earlier and heard about during dinner. "Just wanted to make sure he was good."

"What are your plans today?" I decide to ask my question straight out.

"Well, it's not quite four, and you had mentioned a second round," he answers, walking back to the bed, removing his briefs and sinking a knee onto it as he reaches for his other condom. "Why don't we start there and worry about the rest later?"

I ride him, as he sits with his back to the headboard and gently kisses me, alternating between massaging my breasts or my clit. I may be on top, but Parker still sets the pace and as I am floating back to Earth from my third orgasm of the night, I begin to see the benefits of being with a man who has so much patience.

"Do you mind waiting out here?" Parker asks me as I'm opening my truck door. I raise an eyebrow at him, but shrug and slide back into the driver's seat.

After helping me load up my truck, he wanted to swing by the motel that Ransom stayed in the night before, on our way to breakfast.

That was probably for the best because a few minutes after letting himself into the room, two women file out. My eyes bulge out of my head when one starts to turn in my direction and I all but throw myself down to the floor. It's one of the authors and her PA!

I mean, hey, if that's their thing, more power to them, but I still don't want 'Paige Kyle' hooking up with an older man to be a hot topic in the social media event pages. Even thinking that makes me feel slightly possessive of Parker, not that I have any right to.

Studying the mats, like I now have an opportunity to do, I try to remember the last time I had my truck washed and decide to make time for that sooner rather than later. A loud rap on my window has me strangling down a scream and I pop my head back up.

"Whatcha doing?" Parker asks when I open the window.

"I dropped something," I answer back, but lose my poker face when Ransom's door opens and another woman exits. "Busy bee, isn't he?"

"Yeah, I'm sure he would have appreciated all the condoms you bought," his father answers wryly. "Look, I'm going to secure my things and I'll be ready to go. Ransom will catch up to me later."

"Set your GPS for Stella's Southern Café, if we lose each other we can just meet there," I say, pausing when I wonder if he's thinking about letting things lie here.

At least until he leans through my window and kisses me. "Give me a couple of minutes, then I'll ride on your ass."

"Hmm, we didn't try that position."

"Tease."

With that, he walks back to the room, making two trips before he signals to me that he's ready to go.

Me'ansome - *Now*

Walking into the motel room, I immediately get confirmation that I made the right call in asking Piper to stay in her truck.

Ransom's making out with one woman, another one is giving him head, and the third one is watching as she fingers herself.

"We gotta get on the road," I announce, getting everyone's attention. "Everybody move it along."

Two of the ladies take me seriously, and immediately gather their things, but the watcher slips out of her chair and brings a condom over to my son.

"Seriously, Me'ansome?" My son always switches to my road name when we're among outsiders. "I thought even you would be more relaxed after last night."

"I'm heading to breakfast. Get your ass on the road in the next thirty minutes and share your location with me," I tell him, barely casting a glance when the two women scurry out of the room, before I walk to the adjoining room to make sure none of my shit was messed with and get my things all ready to load up.

When I hear him finishing up with remaining

woman, I take the Joey's books out to my bike before heading over to check on Piper. The last thing I want is for her to get skittish and take off.

The two women that took off together, are just pulling out of the parking lot when I emerge and while Piper's truck is there, she's hidden from sight. I shake my head, grinning at her ass until I finally knock on the window and nearly scare the shit out of her.

The adorable girl tries to lie to me again, but her rosy cheeks give her away and I shake my head at her worries. For all that she's close in age to my kids, she's nothing like them, I think as I head back inside to grab my things and Joey's books.

Not wanting to take a chance on Ransom leaving any of them behind, I load some into the storage compartment on his bike first, slowly double checking that I've left nothing behind, I wonder what the fuck I'm doing.

This is the perfect way to end things. She goes her way, I go mine; albeit, I acknowledge to myself that I've never felt so connected to anyone before.

Piper and me, Christ, this thing I'm feeling doesn't make any sense. But I don't want to ride away from her.

Fuck it. I'll feel her out over breakfast, it's not like I don't have to eat before I hit the road.

"Really?" I prompt her to tell me more as our waffles are delivered.

"Oklahoma has its upsides, but I really wanted the chance to reconnect with Paige once I finished school. And convince her to distance herself from our family," Piper says, once again looking down when she talks about her people. "I think we're good, so I took a month off and I'll scope out areas to move to. I just hope that she'll come with me."

"From the sound of it, the west interests you more than the Gulf Coast? I mean, I think a lot of people your age would look at New Orleans or even Houston." At this point I'm just fishing, trying to get a read on why she's heading west.

"We grew up in Bunkie, Louisiana, so I'm not interested in going back there. Plus, we have a lot of family in Texas and up in New Jersey."

My bullshit detector is on high alert, but I can't tell what she's keeping from me or again, what business it is of mine.

"Now that I got stuck with all of Paige's things from the signing, I'm going to drop them off at home, then strike out on the road. I'll lose a little time, but it's not a big deal," Piper continues.

"Why don't I ride with you?" I blurt that out

without thinking and she looks up at me with her huge brown eyes.

"Sure, I mean, if you want to."

"Just a thought, I didn't mean to put you on the spot, but I am heading back through Dallas also, so it's up to you if you want to put up with me another couple of days."

"What about Ransom?" she asks, carefully pouring more syrup into the squares of her waffle.

"He's a big boy, he can find his way home," I say, grinning as I lean across the table and reaching for a piece of her bacon. "Hey!"

"*My* bacon!" she growls at me, after tapping my hand with her sticky knife.

"Technically, I'm buying breakfast," I stop talking when I see the determined look in her eyes. "Understood. I won't touch your bacon."

"I'm driving up through Lubbock," she quietly tells me.

"Why? That'll add some hours on," I ask, confused at her route.

"I know, but it's safer for me."

With those words, I carefully chew the last bite of my waffle and take a swig of coffee. "You want to explain that to me?"

"No," she says. "That's the way I'm going. I have a hotel reserved for tonight and you're welcome to join me if you want to, but I understand if you don't."

I lean back and nod my head at her. What I want is to have the right to demand she tells me what the fuck is going on, but that's the surefire way to get her to shut down.

The years have taught me to read people and from the little I know about the woman across from me, she values her independence and the more she talks, I'm coming to understand that she has fought, and probably sacrificed, for it.

Me'ansome - *Then*

"Those motherfuckers," Tin growls when I get back from the meeting at my two-bit lawyer's office.

I guess it's either the look on my face or how I reach out for a bottle as I'm passing the bar. Destiny doesn't mess around, she just hands me a handle of rum and I keep walking back to my office.

"What now?" Tin asks, entering through the door I left open and slamming it behind him.

Hearing and feeling the rattle of the wood, almost brings a smile to my face; knowing that one other person feels this as strongly as I do.

"I have her blanket," I tell him. "Jayne didn't even

know to take her favorite one. I keep it in a bag, so it won't lose its smell."

"The one with the monkeys?" he asks and I nod, barely holding it together. The fucking rum isn't helping so I push the bottle away.

"The judge said that the original document she signed isn't valid and then that fucking slick-assed swine sucker presented something that said we decided to split up our fucking children."

Tin turns around and punches his fist through the drywall. It'll just add to the holes I'm made over the past several months.

A knock comes at the door and Nevaeh sticks her head in to tell me that there's a couple cars outside of the gate and they want to talk to me. I nod at her and motion with my hand for her to close the door.

Grabbing the remote control, I turn on the monitors that show all of the cameras around the property.

I quickly focus on the parking lot and see three high-end, black vehicles are parked all in a row and it's as if they know they have my attention, because a man gets out of the passenger side to open the door behind him.

And out steps Jayne's lawyer.

I'm out of my seat, reaching into the cabinet

behind me to arm myself when Tin steps forward to grab my forearm.

"Let's see what they want," he says, his eyes holding mine even as he shakes his head, trying to calm me down. "I'm armed. I'll kill him if you want me to, but Tommy's gonna need you around. Don't let those assholes get both of your kids."

The man has a solid point, I think, exhaling heavily.

"What do you want now?" I yell once I've thrown the door to the clubhouse open. My long stride makes quick work of the distance to the gate.

The window rolls up and a man exits the passenger seat of the second vehicle of their small motorcade, to open the door behind him. Brookhaven's lawyer, Miller, steps out, but through the lightly tinted windows, I notice that there's another man who stays behind.

He's older, his hair is going white, his posture rigid and his countenance disdainful. Like he's just noticed a bit of mud on his expensive shoes. I instantly know this is Jayne's father and I smirk at him. He might think I'm scum, but I'm not the only man around these parts that knows how dirty his daughter likes to play.

His expression never wavers, he merely turns his head to look straight ahead. Deep inside I know that

I haven't won the moment, he wears power like a second skin and nothing that I know about his daughter matters enough to him for him to even raise an eyebrow in my direction.

My eyes flick back to Miller, he's standing just enough to the side so that I could have a clear view of his boss. The other guy continues to the trunk of the vehicle and retrieves a duffle bag.

"Perhaps we could speak inside, Mr. King," the lawyer says, and I realize that in my musings, I had missed something else he had said. Curiosity wars within me so I nod my head and turn on my heel, leading the way back inside.

I retrace my path to my office, ignoring the silence that falls over the room at the sight of the two men behind me. Shaking my head at Destiny, she gets the message not to offer anyone drinks and as the music changes, I see Nevaeh approaching the pole next to the dance floor; which gets my men talking again.

"Again, what do you want?" I repeat my question after sitting behind my large desk.

"Thomas," Miller says, not beathing around the bush. "My client believes the children should be raised together and has the means to give them a very comfortable life."

"They *should* be raised together," I say, in

complete agreement with that part of his statement. "Here, with their father. Where I will provide for them and give them a happy childhood."

I'm having none of it when he opens his mouth to respond.

"Enough! Jayne abandoned them. Even before she left, she didn't give two shits about them. I want to see my daughter, immediately." My voice is firm and I can't help to raise it with each word I speak.

"I'm afraid she's back home, with her caregivers…"

That word nearly makes my control snap. Not with her mother, just with some person they hired.

"Her home is here! Joey needs her family, not some nanny," I bellow. "I don't care how much money that man has, I want my child."

"Trust me when I say, Josephine is very well cared for," Miller says, and looking back at him, I can tell he doesn't give two shits about either child. In fact, he can barely contain his smile.

"She likes to be held when she's going to sleep at night. Does her caregiver know that? She's not picky when it's just a nap, but they have to hold her before bed or she'll howl all night." I don't know why I'm telling him this, it feels like I'm admitting defeat. My eyes are pulled to the man behind him, he sways on his feet and as his mask faulters I instantly know, he has children of his own. "And when she lines up her peas in front of her, she's only going to eat every other one. I don't know why she does that, so they can't get mad at her for wasting the rest. Detergent gives her a rash, not a bad one, but they need to keep an eye on it."

"Have you really given any thought to the pros and cons of this situation, Mr. King?"

I raise an eyebrow in return.

"Mr. Brookhaven is more than willing to compensate you for handing over the boy. *Very generously* compensate you. He'll handle the custody paperwork after that," Miller says. "And you will stay away from them for the rest of their lives."

"And the cons, *Mr. Miller*?"

"The authorities would be given a reason to do a raid here and at your home. After they find, well, whatever they'll be tipped off about, your custody would be striped, I'm sure there would be some jail time—and perhaps it will highlight some issues with your citizenship?" This motherfucker can't hide the glee in his eyes, he's enjoying himself, sitting in my office and bending me over my desk. "Again, it doesn't have to come to that."

"How much is Mr. Brookhaven offering to purchase my son?" I ask him, sitting back in my chair.

"Purchase is such an ugly word…" he starts, but I cut him off.

"You are the one sitting in front of me, while that old bastard sits in the car outside, you don't want to think of yourself as a human trafficker? Well, that's what offering to buy my son makes you!"

"Three million dollars," Miller spits out that number. "I advised against so much, but Mr. Brookhaven wants his grandson pretty badly."

That number knocks the wind out of me, and he waves his hand in the air. The man behind him crosses to my desk and opens the duffle bag, before turning and leaving the room. The disgust was clear on his face.

"Tommy isn't here," I whisper.

"Send your man for him, we'll be waiting in the car," he says before dropping his card on my desk and hurriedly following the guy who was supposed to be his security.

Seconds after he leaves the room, Tin enters it.

"Tell me you got all of that," I plead with him.

He hits a switch on the device in his hand and my voice blares out, "Again, what do you want?"

"You got him to say everyone's name and you said his several times. There won't be any doubt that they tried to buy Thomas, not with this bag here," Tin assures me.

"Think I can trade it back for Joey?" I ask, knowing in my heart they'll never let her go. "And you're sure about this?"

"Make the call, boss," Tin says softly, but steady.

Reaching for Miller's business card, I quickly dial his mobile number.

"Is there a problem, Mr. King?" Miller's voice sounds every bit as assured as it was moments ago and I wish I could see his face.

"Miller, did you know that Utah is a one-party consent state? See, my man, as you called him, got his law degree a couple years back and it's one of those things he's pretty well versed on…"

"I assure you, we have the means to get your audio recording overturned in any court you present it to," he says, trying to intimidate me.

"Yeah, and what about the video, dumbass? Do you want a copy? You detailed Mr. Brookhaven's involvement in the amount of the offer. Copies will be made and if I get so much as a parking ticket, let alone if I don't know where Tommy is for one second of any day going forward, I will flood the internet with it." My voice is shaking, not just with rage, but sorrow. I'm not winning this fight, not so long as they have Joey. "That alone should be enough to get you disbarred."

"And the money? You accepted it," his voice has changed drastically since he last spoke.

"I didn't accept it, you left it here. Come back and get it, it'll be right where your man put it."

With that, the call disconnects and Tin lets out a whistle. "That's a shitload of money right there."

I can't stop the glare I give him, anger coursing through my veins as I try to focus on what we need to do next to protect ourselves.

"Come on, we go to a bank right now, no one else can know about that money. We get a safety deposit box that only the two of us can access. Tommy and Joey are the beneficiaries in case we meet an untimely end."

"That's seeming more and more likely the older we get," Tin grumbles.

"Well, you're welcome to go set up a fucking law practice if that bothers you," I snap back at him, waiting for his response before I continue. As soon as he flips me off, I drop my next bomb. "I need you to take Tommy up to your Grandfather's for a while. I'm going to work on security protocols here and weed out the guys we can't trust."

"How long should I plan on being gone?"

"At least a month. Three million was just his starting point," I tell him. "If they were willing to drop that on my desk and walk out, they'll probably spend twice that the next time they come at us."

"Christ, if some of those guys knew that Tommy was worth a king's ransom, they'd trip over each other trying to kidnap him."

My eyes meet his briefly and, my anger momentarily pushed aside, we share a smirk. "I like it," he says. "Tommy King, Ransom."

"He's a bit young for a road name," I say, even though I can't deny it sounds pretty fucking good.

The next couple months brought the good with the bad.

Fetch was hired on at the Brookhaven estate. He was grumbling about having to oversee the lawn crew when he would have preferred any type of work that involved their numerous vehicles, but by the end of the first month there, he admitted that this way he had more chances to see Joey.

One of the maids, Lina, had been given primary care of my daughter. Finding out about that, we wasted no time investigating her background but found it unlikely that she'd risk her very lucrative position in that household, to moonlight for us.

Especially since several of her family members also worked for the Brookhaven's.

On top of that, I fucking turned my club upside down; making sure that any man left would be willing to die for me. My antics pissed a couple of the guys off enough that they walked, but going forward there would be no room for doubt between any of us.

Tin kept Tommy up at his grandfather's for nearly three months before I felt like anyone slightly interested in what either my brother or the Brookhaven family might have to offer were gone.

I refused to risk leading anyone to them, so I stayed away; missing my children horribly, I drank myself to sleep every night. I was completely uninterested in any of the chicks that hung around the club and cracked down on any of the men hinting at any of our business around them.

In short, I became the grade-A asshole I needed to be to protect my son and my way of life.

FIVE

Me'ansome – *Now*

I take it slow as we pass through the town that Piper lives in. I've got her address programmed in my GPS and decided to give her some space when she pulls up to her house—on the outside chance that her sister made it back or there's any other reason she might want to have a moment there.

This place isn't much different from where I live, being in the middle of the dust bowl, it's less scenic, but looks to be the same kind of town full of people who know each other and are equally willing to lend a hand or mind their own business, whichever is called for in a given situation.

Piper was tense when we got to her hotel room last night and I figured there was only one way to play it. Drop the subject of her family for the time being.

For all I knew, it could have been our last night together, so why mess up a chance to spend it like we did.

Last night she trusted me enough to go for a ride with me, so after spinning around Lubbock for a bit, we settled into a honky-tonk near the hotel and tucked ourselves into a booth.

Nothing's ever felt so natural as keeping my arm draped around her while we talked, ate, and sat back to listen to the band when they began to play. Getting back to the room, I tested her patience a few more times throughout the night. Not bad for a man who feels years older than his age.

Turning into her driveway, I'm not overly surprised to see that hers is the only vehicle around. Piper leaves the front door of her house open as she walks back to her truck, peering into the backseat to appraise the bags and boxes that she neatly packed in the day before.

"Parker, can you grab the books, please?" Piper nods her head to the one box that weighs a ton. That opportunity is too good to pass up, so I promptly put my arms around her to cup each of her breasts in each hand. "Parker!"

"What? You told me to grab your boobs?" I play

dumb as I pull her against my body and start kissing the side of her neck as I gently knead her breasts. "I was going to wait until we got inside, but this is as good a place as any."

She lays her head back against my shoulder, and as a smile slowly spreads across her face, I know I'm in for it.

"You may want to invest in hearing aids, old timer," Piper drawls the words out as she slides her hands down my arms.

"I have them, let me just turn up the volume," I say, giving both of her nipples a quick twist before she figures out where I'm headed.

"Hey!"

"I'm more than willing to kiss them and make them feel better," I promise when she turns within my arms to glare up at me, her forearms braced between our chests. "You know you're not the least bit scary, right? Even when you try to be."

"I'm a little bit scary," she answers, holding the pads of her thumb and pointer finger a smidge apart, right in front of my face.

And I continuously shake my head, right until our lips meet and I wonder how she's managed to turn me upside down in just a few days.

"Terrifying," I concede, pulling back to peck her nose before reaching to pull out the two bags on wheels, before I lift the box she had originally indicated. "What about that other box?"

"Those are the ones I bought and plan on reading along my trip," she answers and I huff at her, still not sure how I feel about this road trip she's going on.

On the one hand, she isn't my woman and rushing into a relationship with someone I don't really know didn't end up so well last time. On the other hand, Piper is either the greatest con-woman ever or she truly can't lie for shit.

Overall, she's pretty fucking perfect in my eyes.

Which can only mean, she'll get a good look at how my life is lived and go running off.

"Parker?" Piper's voice is soft and sounds concerned, when I look over my shoulder at her, realizing she had probably said something to me that I missed.

"Sorry, wool-gathering. Where do you want this?" I ask, slightly lifting the box that's getting heavier by the second.

"Paige's room is the last door on the left," she says, indicating the hallway that connects to the far end of the entrance hall.

"Where's your room?"

"The first on the right."

Looking around, I can tell that most of the décor

is probably how their great-aunt left things, until I get to the hallway and can see it's been freshly painted. Piper's door is just open a crack, so I don't get a look into her room, but notice an updated bathroom just beyond it and some closed doors that are more than likely closets.

Paige must have the master bedroom as it's outfitted with a queen bed, a small couch, and a desk. "Piper, can you come down here?" I call out to her as I set the box on the only clear area of the floor I can find.

"What's wrong?" she asks from the doorway.

"It looks like it was tossed, you should check to see if any valuables are missing," I answer her, confused until I see her try to hide her smile.

"I think she was reorganizing things before she left," Piper says, and it's completely obvious she's covering for her sister.

I try to work together a sentence, some way to inquire about the state of her room, but there's nothing coming to mind that won't get my ass booted out of this house, so I just walk past her and push her door the rest of the way open.

Thank Christ. I let out the breath I didn't realize I was holding until Piper starts to giggle.

"Do I pass inspection?"

"I don't have white gloves with me, but it'll do," I gruffly answer back.

This time she's wrapping her arms around me from behind and I can feel the laughter she's trying to contain.

"You said you two shared a room until you went to college?" I confirm something she mentioned the other night.

"Yeah, she's not all that neat."

"That's the understatement of the year."

"How about you?" Piper lays her head against my back as I stand still, my eyes scanning her room as I catalog the things she obviously holds special.

"Growing up, I was your typical boy, I guess, but fatherhood made me understand the value of keeping a tidy home," I tell her. "Did you lock up your truck?"

"Yes," she says, circling under my arm to stand in front of me. "And the front door."

"Good girl." Leaning down to kiss her.

"I even changed my sheets before I left home."

"That's so fucking hot," I mock-growl at her, loving the sound of her laughter before I bend over enough to loop my arm behind her knees and carry her to the bed.

Piper

Two condoms my ass, Me'ansome seems to have an endless supply of them, I think as he rolls one down his length. Not that I'm complaining.

"You know, this would be a lot easier if you weren't grinning at me like that," he says, not even looking at me as he focuses on the task at hand.

"I'm happy to lend a hand," I sass back, unable to hold in my giggle. "Sorry, your reaction to Paige's room cracked me up."

"Why don't you flip over onto your knees and maybe later I'll compliment you on how neat you are," he tells me before lunging at me.

"What happened to 'patience'?" I squeal, pretending that I'm trying to get away from him. Not that it makes a difference, Parker easily spins me around to position me doggy style.

His lips hit the base of my neck, giving me shivers as he kisses his way up to my earlobe. "I can't get enough of you," he whispers, guiding his cock in between my folds before reaching up to knead my breast.

Parker's first thrust is rougher than I'm used to from him and my eyes widen in surprise. Bracing myself firmly against the headboard, I turn back to look at him as he continuously drives into me.

It's the look he's giving me that sets my blood on fire, pushing me to buck my hips back against his thrusts, faster and faster. When he slides a finger down to flick my clitoris, my orgasm suddenly sweeps through me and I collapse my forehead down to the bed unable to stop the trembles that have overtaken my body.

His cock continues to churn up and down my passage until I feel it twitching and tighten myself around him, not relenting even after he swears and swats at my ass before half collapsing on top of me.

"I don't want to move," he says, tightening his arm around me to keep me as close as possible to.

"I'm good," I needlessly assure him as he starts to lightly snore in my ear.

Lying beside Parker, I listen to the steady rhythm of his breathing and push back his dark hair that has fallen across his forehead. I start to trace the lines on his forehead before yanking my hand back, not wanting to creep him out if it wakes him up.

Instead, I just study his face, as I wonder how our one-night stand has turned into three nights and nearly jump when I feel his stomach rumble where our flesh is pressed together.

Damn. I'd emptied out the fridge before I left, knowing that Paige won't bother to cook anything if she's by herself. Which I'll never understand, because of the two of us, she's definitely the more gifted in that category.

"Come to Utah with me," Parker's voice is low and rough with sleep, yet clear nonetheless and I can't contain the smile that spreads across my face.

"What if we implode in a few days and what could be left as a happy memory..." my sentence is cut off by his lips pressing firmly to mine.

"What time is it?" he asks.

"Probably close to seven," I guess, looking out of the window to gage the remaining light.

"We be honest," Parker's voice remains low as if he's trying to stay calm, and he reaches up to cup my cheek. "Seven, every morning and night, we tell each other if this is working or not. We respect each other enough to part on good terms if it isn't."

The idea leaves me momentarily speechless; it's straightforward enough that it might actually work. "Is that something you've tried before?"

"Nope. I'm just making shit up on the fly, in the hopes of getting a little more time with you, Piper," he says, his forehead resting against mine.

"I still have my list of areas I want to check out. Would you be interested, or able, to come with me to some of them?" I ask, cringing when I realize that qualifies as planning past the 'twelve hours at a time' deal he suggested. When I peek up at his face, his smile tells me everything I need to know.

"We can make that work, if you'll ride with me." My eyes widen and I wonder how that'll work on his motorcycle for days on end, but that is not a *today problem*.

"I don't have any food in the house," I blurt out when I feel his stomach rumble again, feeling more comfortable making short-term plans over long-term ones. For now, at least.

Getting dressed, I worry about having to, potentially, tell him about my family. The more we have talked over the past few days, has painted a clearer picture of how deep his roots are to the small town he lives in and while I know I'm missing part of the story about his kids, being close to Ransom and Joey means a lot to him.

I can't imagine ever feeling safe enough to stay in any place for very long. Any little thing could set off my mom or her siblings into coming after me for what they think is owed to them. Cursing Paige for continuing to do jobs for them on the downlow, I start to think that even considering going to Utah with him could put his children in their crosshairs.

Me'ansome – *Then*

"This is hell," Fetch said during his monthly check-in.

Admittedly, it has been a rough few months. By this time, he had moved on from the Brookhaven estate and was happily working a maintenance gig at Joey's grammar school and was in regular contact with her caretaker.

Jayne's father unexpectedly dropped dead and, nearly overnight, she shipped Joey off to a boarding school. No matter how tough the old man had proven with his protection protocols over the past decade, Jayne, and her new husband, proved just as fierce.

Lina, the maid who had practically raised my daughter didn't even know where Joey had been sent and was beside herself with worry. Luckily, their closeness was the silver-lining that finally brought us the needed information. Joey was able to get to a phone one day and called Lina sobbing, miserable in her new surroundings.

It brought me some comfort to know she had been raised with a woman who cared for her, even though Lina was powerless to protect Joey's life from being uprooted. Not by her mother, of course, but at least she had formed a strong bond with someone more down to Earth than any of the Brookhavens.

Thankfully, Lina considered Fetch her confidant, and I suspect her boyfriend also, so she wasted no time in letting him know where Joey was and the next day we started working on his new alias. His background was padded enough to get him a job at the prestigious school, without raising eyebrows about a man who had spent over a decade working either for the family or the previous school, of their newest transfer student.

"Fetch, you've done more for me than I ever expected, I can't ask you to keep up this…"

"Fuck off, Me'ansome." That he is invoking my road name, meant that I hit a nerve and just wait on him to continue. "Your mom was better to me than my own and if your daughter has to suffer through this, I'm not leaving her. Just, I haven't seen Joey cry since she was a toddler, but these entitled mother-fuckers are giving her hell."

"Is it time to *extract* her?" I ask him for, what must be, the thousandth time. He and I both know that if I do that then I have to grab Tommy and try to hide the three of us at the furthest corner of this planet.

The only part of the three million I've ever touched was to feed into an account for Fetch. While the Brookhavens paid him handsomely, I know the kind of loyalty and dedication he's given me has cost him in many ways.

"No." I may be Joey's father, but Fetch's voice is determined. "I don't care about the last name on her paperwork, she's a *motherfucking* King. Joey will rise above all of these snot-nosed assholes and it will make her stronger."

I can barely choke out my thanks before I hang up. The guilt I feel for losing my daughter eats at me every night. I love and am proud of the man Tommy is becoming, yet I know I've fucked up by keeping so much of this history from him.

The problem is, he's as much a hot-head as I was at that age—and I know goddamn well, what his mother's rebellious stage led to—so until Joey graduates from high school and I can introduce myself to her, Tin and I have held fast to our decision to keep him from finding out about Joey.

I send a silent nod to the Fates, in thanks for gifting me with a small group of friends that I know will always have my back. The three of them almost make up for the shit I've gone through due to Parson. To a point.

Fetch, my cousin Mark, my twin brother, and I grew up on an estate, referred to as subdivisions in the States, on the edge of Truro, Cornwall. If there was any trouble in the area, we were the first ones everyone went looking for. As we hit our teenage years, Fetch, Mark, and I grew more and more weary of Parson's nature; which resulted in hanging out with him less and less.

By that time, Fetch's mom was on her third husband, an abusive asshole who didn't want step-children hanging around. His older sister went to live with her grandparents, but no one raised an eyebrow when he moved into our two-bedroom place; keeping his clothes in a duffle bag in the room I shared with Parson and sleeping on the couch.

Mom didn't make much and the government pension that was part of my father's death benefit was stretched thin as it was, but we made do. In all honesty, he'd been staying at our place more than his own by the time he was ten.

The years leading up to my sixteenth year really should have prepared me for what was coming. Parson was hanging with kids from an older gang and missing school most days, being ten times smarter than any of them, he quickly rose through their ranks.

Being his identical twin sucked because I was the

one the rozzers could actually locate and they would regularly pick me up when shopkeepers gave a description of who had knocked over their store, or when the occasional girl was brave enough to lodge a complaint over being held down and groped.

Staying in school and doing odd jobs throughout the town, at least gave me a solid alibi on some of those days, but Parson's antics led to me spending too much time at the local station, until my mom or our parish priest could come and verify that I was Parker and not Parson.

It was shortly after our sixteenth birthday, and I'll never forget the day—Mark and I were standing in line to get into the trilogy of Star Wars movies playing at the local theater when no less than five police cars pulled up and I knew two things instantly.

They were there for me and Parson had done something much more serious than selling drugs or stealing a few quid.

Looking at Mark, I said the only thing that came to mind. "Make sure that Fetch watches out for Mum."

And I ran. Ducking behind the others standing in line, I made it to the corner and hi-tailed it out of there as fast as I could. A few blocks away, I heard one of the rozzers calling out for me to stop just as the delivery boy for the local grocer pulled up on his bike.

We shared a look and he obviously saw how desperate I was.

"Hit me first, mate," he said, his eyes indicating that his keys were still in the ignition. I had recognized him from around town, but we had gone to different schools so had never spoken before. The moment I punched him I wished I knew his name.

"I owe ya," I whispered, by way of thanks and made off with, what was probably his pride and joy, a fully gassed up piece of shit motorcycle.

Barely thinking of a destination, I headed south to the closest port. Two days before, my father's best mate had stopped in for a visit. They had served together, but for the past several years he had been with the merchant mariners, and I prayed that his ship was still in port.

One thing was for certain, this fucking island was too small for the twin King brothers and I had had enough.

I stayed on that ship for nearly two years, only occasionally setting my feet on dry land since I didn't have any papers. It was when we were docked just south of Los Angeles that the man I came to see as a surrogate father handed me an envelope containing

U.S. dollars, a passport, and a social security number.

More than anything, I was touched that I was able to keep the name my parents had given me. My accent had long since faded so my name was the only thing I had left from home.

Heading inland, away from the sea, I enjoyed spending time in a dryer climate and eventually met Tin over a game of pool and fell in with his construction crew.

SIX

Me'ansome - *Now*

As I've done for years, I wake up early and fish around for my briefs before I tuck the blankets around Piper and hit the bathroom.

If I were at home, I'd get a workout in, but I settle for getting a mug of coffee instead. Piper had explained that they recently had the kitchen renovated and since they intend to sell the house, hadn't bothered to unpack things; choosing to leave a few things out instead. With Paige in the wind, I snag one of the two mugs in sight and turn on the K-cup machine.

As the last few drops sputter out, I hear another noise that doesn't make sense in this sparsely populated area and bring my coffee with me when I go to look out the large bay window near the front door.

Sure enough, there's a car idling in front of the house. The headlights are turned off and through the faint, early-morning light I can see three figures all looking back at me. There's at least one man, though I can't accurately describe the other two people in the car.

I do know it's a little fucking early to be flipped off, which is what that man does before the car makes a U-turn on the otherwise empty road.

The thought that nags at me is how Piper insisted I pull my motorcycle into the small garage last night and what level of trouble she might be in—or if this morning's company was looking for Paige instead.

Knowing Piper for less than four days at this point, and sure as fuck not having opened up about my personal shit, I can hardly expect her to confide in me, but I will insist on it if I catch wind of anything else.

There is one thing I can do and that's text Diesel. He's a member of the Royal Bastards with Axel back in Flagstaff and mighty talented when it comes to digging shit up online. I give him the girls' names and current address, before I finish the rest of my coffee and go to brew one for Piper.

It's close enough to seven when I wake her. At

least, I'd like to think it was my kisses more than the smell of the coffee that entices her to do more than crack open her second eye and stop snarling.

"You're so damn cute in the morning," I tell her, suddenly unsure that it's the best time to confirm that she wants to stick with me a bit longer.

"Parker?"

"Hmm?"

"I can't have sex with you now," she says, blowing on the coffee she's holding with both hands. "Maybe tonight, but I may have bitten off more than I can chew these past few nights."

"Babe, I know you're not awake yet, but please don't ever use that phrase in any sentence that vaguely references my dick," I tell her, sliding my hand over my package. Her snort blows little waves onto the surface of the drink and her eyes flash with laughter.

"Do you still want me to follow you to Utah?"

"I'm really hoping you will, Piper."

"Can we stop at the Four Corners?" she asks and while it'll add some time onto the trip, I remind myself that she's supposed to be on vacation.

"If we leave in the next half hour, we can be there by mid-afternoon and sleep at my house tonight."

With that, she throws back her coffee and flies around the room getting ready to leave.

"Hey, Dad, where's your spare key?" Joey's voice feeds through my headset and I frown, trying to figure out why she's not home in bed.

"How is your recovery going? Where's Axel?"

"I'm good, Tommy said you had a surprise for me and I'm losing my mind at home so I convinced Axel that I can sit around, doing nothing at your house, just as easily as I can at ours."

That traitorous little bastard. Like his godfather, once Tommy gets on the road, he prefers to push straight through, and once home he couldn't help but tease Joey into coming up for a visit.

It must have been the long months I spent at sea, but for me, life was more about the journey than the destination.

"It's not that kind of surprise," I tell her. "I met someone and she's going to stay with me for a couple of days. Maybe longer."

"Ohmygod," the words fall from her lips in a jumble before she screams out. "Axel, you have to get us a hotel room."

"Honey, you're already there and we won't get in until late, but yeah, I wouldn't mind a little privacy after tomorrow. Besides, you can pick up the rest of your books this way and *stay off* your feet while you read them."

"It's not you, Axel." Joey's obviously talking to both of us at once and her voice suddenly changes to a sing-song tone, to give me shit. "Daddy's got a girlfriend. Oh, wait, what do you call it when you're older? Lady friend?"

If it was anyone else, I'd tell them to fuck off; it's just that my relationship with Joey is still untested in some ways so I tell her where to find the hidden key and drop the call.

Thankfully, when Piper and I pull up to my house later that night, the only sign of Joey and Axel is their SUV parked outside of my garage. It had been a long day on the road, and while I know Piper was nervous about meeting Joey, at least she'll be able to do it with a full night's rest under her belt.

Piper

I'm more than a little surprised that I wake up before Parker, but nature called and while I considered hiding out in his room, I didn't like feeling like a coward.

"Oh! I'm sorry! Shit."

When confronted with a humongous, nearly naked man in the kitchen, the words fly out of my mouth even as I consider running back to Parker's room.

"Who are you?" His deep voice isn't unkind, even though it's definitely filled with surprise.

"Who are you?" I parrot back to him, leaving the two of us staring at each other. Which is good because then I'm not looking at the collection of tattoos across his naked chest or the towel that's barely clinging to his hips.

"Axel," Parker's voice directly behind me alerts me to his presence approximately three seconds before his hand curls around me and lands on my stomach, pulling me back against his chest.

"Parker," the giant greets him in a similar tone as a huge grin splits his face and one of his eyebrows arches up. "Now this explains why Tommy and Tin wouldn't answer any of Joey's questions."

"What?" I ask, putting my hands on my hips and pulling myself up to my full height.

"What?" Axel parrots my question back to me.

"What 'explains why'?" I clarify my question.

"I'll go get Joey, she'll want to know you set up a playdate for her." Axel says, looking over my head so I know his comment is directed toward Parker.

If not for the added pressure Parker puts against my stomach, I wouldn't have noticed that I had started toward the giant jerk—who's at least smart enough to exit the kitchen on the other side of the island.

"Don't take it personal, sweetheart. I've given him a ton of shit for robbing the cradle by marrying my daughter," he purrs in my ear. "Besides, I don't think it'd be a fair fight."

That takes some of the wind out of my sails before I'm filled with doubt about us. We've been in our own bubble up until now, but the harsh reality of Axel's words, even if he was just giving his father-in-law a hard time, weigh on me.

"Where's your head, Piper?" he asks as I stay frozen in his arms. "It's already past seven, so if you want to call it a day, you can skip meeting Joey.

"I don't, do you? No, but it might still be too early for a family day," Me'ansome says with a soft smile. "Want me to tell them to hit the road?"

"No, because I don't get the impression that your family is anything like my family. If you want me here, then it's important that I get to know Joey," I tell him and he leans down to kiss me.

"I agree," a woman's voice comes from behind the man in my arms and he lets out a large sigh against my mouth. Peeking around him, there's no mistaking the green eyes that eagerly study my face.

"Can you bring the books in?" I ask Me'ansome

before tearing my eyes away from his daughter—damn, this man makes good looking children—to see him staring down at my boobs and my face flames red. I silently mouth 'Don't' as a warning, hoping he won't embarrass me in front of his daughter.

"Axel," he calls out. "Piper's keys are on the table next to the door, go grab the two boxes from the backseat of her truck.

"Two boxes?" Axel grumbles. "How many books did you buy, Joey?"

"Oh, most of what's in there are my books," I say, lightly stepping on Parker's foot so he'll shift his eyes up from the point of my V-neck shirt as I try to cover for the woman who's only a few years younger than me. "But I packed them together to save space."

"And this is after Tin and Tommy dropped other books off." Axel doesn't look convinced by my excuse. He's still standing behind her with his arms crossed, but has thankfully thrown on some clothes.

"Thirty, like we agreed," Joey answers her husband, giving me a quick wink, and for the first time I notice the crutches she's leaning on.

"I thought you said twenty?"

"I pre-ordered twenty originally, and we both know I was going to buy more books the day of the signing, so I added some more." With that Axel lets out a huff and turns to go out to retrieve the boxes.

"Don't mind him, he's surprising me with a specially made bookcase and doesn't want to have to change the order."

"Oh! That's so thoughtful!" I respond, having felt awkward listening to their exchange.

"Don't tell him that I know, but I saw him measuring some other books I have and there's a spot in our living room that he wouldn't let me move the couch to when I rearranged the furniture."

"Tell me you didn't rearrange the furniture after you took your tumble?" Parker asks Joey, drawing up to his full height as he turns toward her.

"Are you kidding? Axel would have duct taped me to a chair if I had tried that," she responds, rolling her eyes before looking back at me. "I'm sorry, I don't know your name."

"I'm Piper. My sister is an author, Paige Kyle, and your dad actually bought one of her books for you," I tell her, as her dad grunts in agreement with her statement about her husband, before I nod to the living room. "Would you be more comfortable sitting down? Do you want something to drink?"

"You two go on," Parker says, patting me on the ass when I turn to follow her over to the couches.

Within minutes, Joey and I are shooting off the names of our favorite authors and books, barely acknowledging Axel when he puts the boxes on the coffee table and retreats back to the kitchen.

"Can I ask…"

"Twenty-four," I tell Joey how old I am without looking up as I sort through the books.

"I don't know if he told you much, but I wasn't raised here. I didn't know him until I was eighteen and granted, it's only been a few years, but I've never seen him with anyone before." Joey furrows her brow when she looks over her shoulder as if figuring out how much she should say. "Not that I think he's a monk or anything, but it means something that he brought you home. Keep that in mind, alright?"

Well, if I didn't have questions before, I sure as hell do now.

SEVEN

Me'ansome – *A few years ago*

"Me'ansome." The tone of Tin's voice tells me I'm not going to enjoy this call. Considering their run-in with the Royal Bastards the other day, I just hope Ransom cooled his jets.

"What?"

"Sit down." Tin's words strike fear into my soul. I'm trying to track my daughter down and all I can suddenly imagine is that something's happened to Tommy. "Joey's here. Red pieced it together and was going to tell Ransom, thankfully I shut that shit down and got him out of the room. She found out about you when she graduated and came out to…"

"Joey's with you?" I am fucking glad I took his

advice, as my brain feels like it's been submerged in ice water and my heart rate is off the charts. "Is she?"

"Alright, I gotta track Ransom down, he doesn't know yet, so fucking listen and we'll talk later because I have zero details." Tin doesn't leave any room for argument and I'm still in shock from hearing that Joey came looking for me. "She's a Royal Bastard's Ol' Lady—Axel. Don't know how the fuck that happened, but he's glued to her, inked her up and all. He said she got picked up—possibly by Parson, and left with traffickers. And I quote, '*She wasn't brutalized but made to witness it*'. You're to call Declan and set up conditions to meet her."

I hang up and sit up straight in my chair. If Tin said he had zero details, I know he meant it.

Leaning over, I put my head between my knees and pray to a God that I've spent years cursing out. Begging him that the shortness of breath and contractions I'm feeling isn't a heart attack, that I can't be this close to seeing my baby girl and die right now.

Shit. Declan and I have been on the outs lately, but I'll say whatever I need to if it means getting to see my daughter as soon as fucking possible.

Taking a deep breath, I reach for the landline and call him.

"Can't talk right now," Declan growls out without preamble.

"You can't keep me from her, you asshole," I bark back at him, instantly forgetting my resolve to play nice, and hear him exhale.

"Not my intention," he says after a moment. "I got other shit going on. Call me tomorrow."

Instead of waiting around to call him back, I go to pack a bag, needing to get to Flagstaff so I'll be in range of Joey.

Of all the ways I pictured reuniting with my daughter, seeing her charge into the Bastards' strip club looking for her Ol' Man was not on the list. Joey's expression went from anger to embarrassment the moment she realized there wasn't a woman in sight. And while I nearly leapt out of my seat at the sight of her, I realized that playing it cool would serve me best.

I also realized that, as new as her relationship with Axel was, she had some serious feelings for him already. Sitting back with a smirk on my face, I was proud of the fact that if she thought her man was doing something wrong, she wasn't going to run away and lick her wounds. Nope, my little girl had barged in here, all spit and vinegar, ready to do battle.

She's a fucking King, all right.

Once Axel calmed her down, we continued our meeting to patch things up between our clubs and he invited me over for dinner that night. I didn't miss the shit-eating grin that Declan shot him, mocking him for having to welcome me as family because none of that mattered to me.

What mattered was a few hours later, after cleaning up the mess she'd made in the kitchen and laying my cards on the table, my little girl and I found the peace we both needed from each other. When she hugged me goodnight, I never wanted that moment to end.

Me'ansome - *Now*

"Is she older or younger than Joey?" Axel asks me when he reenters the kitchen.

"What the fuck were you doing naked in my kitchen this morning?" I counter.

"Showered, after I worked out," he shrugs, unable to keep the smirk off his face. "Never known you to miss a workout, but I guess she's wearing you out, huh? I know a guy that can get you the blue pills, no shame in asking. Just be careful you don't wind up with a dad-bod."

I take a step toward him when the backdoor opens and Ransom walks through carrying a couple of containers of food with him.

"Tin's behind me with the rest of it," he announces with a grin that nearly matches Axel's. "Is my new mommy here? Are you making it official?"

"Get the fuck out of my house," I tell them just as Tin is putting one foot over the threshold.

"Dad?" Joey gently calls to me from the living room. "Axel and Tommy, you two knock it off. Let's sit down for breakfast, then we'll get out of your hair."

From the corner of my eye, I see Ransom open his mouth, but Tin kicks out at his knee, effectively getting him to keep his comments to himself.

"Where's Piper?" I ask my daughter who's keeping her glare focused on her husband. She points in the direction of my bedroom and I head off in search of Piper.

"Calm down, Paige." I hear her voice before I see her standing near the window, holding her phone up to her ear. "What did you think was going to happen, working for them again?"

Piper pinches the bridge of her nose as she listens to her sister and I debate revealing my presence.

"No, I haven't seen any of them," and "I heard 'Ballad for a Friend' the other day, remember how we used to love that one?" are the next things she says to the infamous Paige and I cock my head to the side, trying to figure out what she's talking about.

Especially since I don't have any hint as to what's going on.

Clearing my throat, I enter the room, disappointed to see her shoulders stiffen as she continues to listen to her sister and occasionally mention song titles or movies.

Hmm, I pull out my phone and search for 'Ballad for a Friend', quickly finding out it's a Bob Dylan song that references Utah. Damn, the two of them are having a secondary conversation that flows under the superficial one that I'm listening to.

I would be impressed, if it wasn't completely fucked up, that she and her sister had to devise the system in the first place.

Laying down on my bed, I can't help but grin

when Piper stops her pacing and snuggles up along-side me before wrapping up the call.

"Everything alright?"

"No," she answers, burrowing into my shoulder.

"Can I help?"

"No. But I don't think I'm long-term relationship material either," Piper truly sounds forlorn when she says this, at least I tell myself that to keep my stomach from dropping.

"Honey," I say, hooking my finger under her chin to get her to look up at me. "My twins are your age, my ex-wife abandoned them then came back and kidnapped Joey when she was an infant, now it turns out she and her current husband are involved in human trafficking. Plus, you may have noticed, I'm the President of a motorcycle club and there ain't a choir boy among us."

"Our family raised Paige and I to run cons. Small ones at first, but they were just training us to execute bigger heists. I basically ran away from home to go to college and my legitimate job makes me the black sheep of the family," she confesses, almost sounding like she's trying to top what I had just said.

"My brother got involved with some serious fucking people from south of the border. Who also happened to be into human trafficking—he picked

Joey up before she could get to me. She wasn't hurt, but she was meant to be auctioned off. He failed."

"Permanently?" Piper asks, pulling her finger across her throat and I nod. "I think they're using some threat against me to keep Paige working for them. She won't admit it, but it's my fault."

With that, she starts to cry; holding her arm across her face as if to shield me from her tears.

"If you'll let me talk this over with Tin and Axel, maybe we can figure out a way to get you and Paige free of this?" I ask for her permission, regardless of the fact that I already had Diesel looking into her background.

"Ugh, Axel is a beast. And no, I don't want your family in danger because of me."

"Axel might be a bit rough around the edges, but can you imagine what he's like when he's on your side?" I ask and she lets out a hiccup.

"It won't help much now. Paige said that she needs until the end of the year for whatever it is she's doing. That means I won't hear from her for a few months."

"Maybe someday you'll explain this coded system you two have worked out?" I ask her and she shakes her head, giving me the first smile in a while.

"I can't break the *other* code," she whispers, desperately trying not to grin. "Chicks before dicks."

I bark out a laugh, never having heard that one before. "Speaking of which, how are you feeling down there?"

"Must you look so pleased with yourself?" she asks me in reply, before wiggling down my body.

"Babe, we've got company," I half-heartedly mumble as she tugs on the button and lowers the zipper of my jeans.

"I promise, I won't make a sound," Piper says with a wink as she pulls my dick out and swirls her tongue around the ridges.

Sucking me in, she pulls her mouth back with a pop and I let out a low moan.

"Shh," she hushes me, holding my dick in front of her lips like a finger before she starts licking the underside of it.

"Brat."

Bending my knees to almost cradle her body, I reach down and thread my fingers through her silky, dark hair. Piper seems to enjoy the light pressure I put on her as she works her head up and down my cock, slathering and sucking me off with relentless enthusiasm.

"I'm gonna explode." At my words, she slides even further down my length until I'm hitting the entrance to her throat, barely giving me a chance to pull back into her mouth before my release spills into her mouth. "Oh, fuck, baby."

It's when she gives one final lick from the base to the end of my dick, like I'm her favorite flavor of ice cream, that I know I'm done. I need this woman in my life and fucked up family or not, I'll do whatever needs to be done to be able to keep her by my side.

EIGHT

Piper

There were knowing looks all around when we emerged from Parker's room, with the exception of Joey who couldn't seem to make eye contact with me for a while.

Of the group, it is Tin who I find to be the most disconcerting. He never seems to be very far from me and his eyes are always following me. What's more, I feel like he's weighing and cataloging each word I speak.

"Piper, do you think you could convince your sister to come for a visit sometime? I'd love to get a chance to talk to her about her books, once I get to read her titles."

"Oh, I can try," I hedge, my eyes looking over to

meet Parker's, but notice he and Tin are talking about something.

"And I don't know if she's interested, but last summer I got to meet another author. Her name's Sophia, her Old Man is in the Northern Grizzlies up in Idaho. They might know each other already from social media, anyway I just love her stories and world building."

"Oh! I know who you're talking about," I tell her, happy to have a safe topic to talk about. One that doesn't involve my love life. "I actually handle most of Paige's social media, so I met her—online, at least —she's super sweet."

"Do you and Paige look much alike?" Ransom asks, looking up at me with an odd expression on his face.

I hadn't even noticed Tin and Parker coming up behind me and without warning, the next thing I know, Tin is knocking Ransom upside the head while I hear his dad cursing and Axel's booming laugh rings out.

"That's fucking twisted, man," Axel says, shaking with laughter.

I just look around the room, trying to figure out everyone's reaction until I see the blush on Joey's face and remember seeing the two women leaving Ransom's room the other morning.

"My brother's a perv. Just ignore him," she mumbles.

The next few weeks are among the happiest of my life and while I've been checking in with my boss to keep up to date on upcoming projects, I really just enjoy the time I've spent on the road with Me'ansome.

A friend of his has an HD Touring bike that he's been loaning us for our trips, and I have to say, I'm more than a little in love with it.

The longest trip we took was up to the Sturgis and Deadwood area of South Dakota and while I could live there in a heartbeat, my heart is very much stuck in one place right now.

We had another trip up through Utah and into Idaho, where I got to meet Sophia as we stayed with a past President of the Northern Grizzlies MC, Flint. And that in itself was an eye-opener. Showing me, clearer than any discussion would have, that even if Me'ansome turned the reigns of his MC over to Ransom, he'd still be an active member.

But it was hearing the Northern Grizzlies reliving details of shoot-outs they had with rival groups that started to shake me out of the bubble we'd been living in.

Seeing how Me'ansome sat back and watched me absorb the stories of various members' deaths or torture, made me understand that these were things he lived with also. He was part of a world that was possibly more violent than the one I had fled at my first opportunity.

Me'ansome – *Now*

I've *very* recently come to understand that the best feeling in the world is closing your eyes and then, hours later, opening them next to—well, in my case, Piper. I'm sure this isn't an unheard-of phenomenon; I had just never experienced it before.

Diesel was pretty quick to get back to me with information on the shit-show that counts as Piper and Paige's family. Granted, Paige is nearly as dirty as the rest of them. Or at a minimum, holds most of their secrets in her own blood-stained hands.

At the end of the day, Paige's love for her sister is also her redeeming quality—and not a trait that runs deep in that family. From what Diesel pieced together, we decided that Paige staying 'in the fold' was the price for their mother not sending out a search party for Piper, when she made her run for it.

If there were ever any people I'd want to burn to the ground, Piper's family is now running neck and neck with the Brookhavens.

In my world, trust is more important than any emotion. And I trust Piper.

I trust her so much, I gave her a debit card linked to my accounts—we had gone from a one-night stand to living together in the space of a few days. Regardless of how successful she is as a consultant, I insisted on covering groceries and gas for my household. Since she has my extra house and car keys, what does my bank card matter?

For the first time since I'd known him, Tin didn't comment. Which I took as his approval, but that was another tricky subject. Luckily, one that a big-ass bottle of Jameson helped to solve.

"I saw her in your arms that night after the author event, man, and the sight of her took my breath away," Tin told me and my stomach knotted up like it never had before. "I've watched you two ever since you brought her back here. And I know, I know she's not the one for me, but goddamn, if I coulda pictured the woman for me, Piper, looks-wise, would be it."

"Yeah, thanks for that, you shithead," I laughed, more than half in the bag myself.

"But she's not it. Not for me. She's, well, she's like a chess player and I'm like the guy at the fair with that sledge hammer who rings a bell," he slurred out and I shook my head.

"I've seen you win too many court cases to listen to this pity party," I scoffed back at him.

"How I do my job ain't the same as how I want to live my life. Piper, she's beautiful, but her personality and mine would never fit. Not like you two do."

Throwing back the whiskey in my glass, I grabbed the bottle to pour us two more as I changed the topic to our good old times.

Tin and I talked into the early morning hours and I kept tossing about what I had learned about Paige, and the thought of Piper having a mirror image out in the world made me grin. I also recognized it put me on Ransom's level to think that the man whom I considered my brother might possibly connect with her sister in the way she and I have.

Lately, Piper has consumed most of my days and all of my nights. Between our road trips and time spent with my kids, and Axel—who I am grudgingly including into my family circle, I know I'm all in with Piper.

My heart is at least.

Then again, my brain is screaming that I was just a couple years younger than she is now when I ran off to Vegas with Jayne, all of three minutes after we figured out she was pregnant.

We have kept our promise to each other, but instead of any sort of conversation, one of us generally kiss the other at seven A.M. or seven P.M. In our own special way, it's like having two anniversaries a day.

"Babe?" I call out when I get home with our dinner. Piper's muffled reply comes from the table on the back patio and I smile when I see she's set it up for our dinner, including a small cooler with my favorite beer next to the chair she's pointing at for me.

"You're late and I'm starving," she says by way of greeting and I hand off the bag to her while I quickly go to wash my hands.

"Welcome home," Piper leans her face up for a kiss when I return.

"Did you skip lunch?"

"No, I ate earlier, I'm just really hungry," she replies and from the mountain of food she dished up for herself, I begin to wonder if I ordered enough.

"I wanted to talk to you about something," I

start, worried how she's going to take the news since her eyes were opened up a bit more than I had planned during our trip to Idaho.

"You're not allowed to break up with me until seven," she squeals, holding her hand out to stop me. "Those are the rules."

"I thought we agreed I wasn't stupid?" I ask, raising my brow at her as she continues to eat. "A work thing came up, so I have to go away for a few days; a week tops."

Piper doesn't say anything out loud, but I can practically hear the thoughts running through her mind.

"You've got the run of the house, of course, and if you want, I can ask Joey to come stay with you. Axel will probably be with her if she does," I add, hoping she'll say something soon.

"I think I'll head up to Spokane and visit my college roommate if you're going to be gone," she says, her eyes focused on the food in front of her.

"You're not allowed to break up with me until seven, sweetheart," I remind her, my voice rough with longing.

"I'm not breaking up with you, Me'ansome." The sincerity in her eyes calm me down a little. "But I don't know what we're doing and I don't want to overstay my welcome."

Pushing my chair back, I reach over and yank Piper out of hers to settle her on my lap. "I want every moment you'll give me, sweetheart. If you want me to put your name on the deed, I will. I have no idea what you're doing with me and I honestly thought you'd run after some of the stories you heard. You still being here has given me hope, that you can live with that part of me. Am I wrong?"

"No, it's just been such a whirlwind and I keep waiting for something to blow-up. I think I just need this solo trip to get my head straight."

If she wasn't pushing herself deeper into my embrace I'd probably be on the verge of vomiting my dinner. What I know about Piper, is that she had to nurture herself and her sister from the time she was a toddler. Despite that, she has a huge heart and if this is what she needs to put us into perspective, I have to trust that she'll come back to me.

No matter how much I fucking hate it.

"So, this college roommate of yours, it's a woman, right?" I ask, only having heard the name Dani and hoping it's not a 'Danny', instead. "And married?"

"Yes, *she's* married and a librarian, so there won't be any wild nights out. Unlike you," she answers, tapping me on the nose with her finger. "Now, let me finish my dinner then you can demonstrate your *patience* for me to remember while we're apart."

"I'm gonna be so goddamn *patient* with you," I promise, reaching to pull her plate over so she can finish eating from her spot on my lap.

Being the more mature of the two of us, I wait until she takes another bite before I cup and start kneading her breasts. God, I fucking love her tits.

NINE

Piper

After taking the most winding route I could from southern Utah up to Spokane, I spent the first couple of days feeling absolutely carefree as I caught up with my friend and got to know her husband.

My next project at work is slated to start up the following Monday, so I will have to take up Parker's offer to use one of his spare bedrooms as a home office. Home offices is the new normal in the world, so as long as I have internet, I can honestly work from anywhere. Of course, now, my head is spinning with another use for one of the other rooms.

There are so many things that made me wish Parker was here with me. Due to the nature of his business, we had agreed on a schedule to speak to each other and I decided I hated that more than anything, even if it made me co-dependent. I have just gotten so used to him being with me and how we can talk about anything, or nothing and just enjoy each other's nearness.

I had made up my mind that was I going to leave a few days early so I could cut across the state and drive down the coast to San Francisco before going home. I smiled and hoped that I really had found my home with Parker, and that my news will be welcome.

But I need to make one more stop before leaving Spokane.

And that's how I found myself wandering the aisles of a Safeway market, at least until I realized I had picked up a tail. The acne faced teenager, with a store issued name badge, wasn't even discreet about following me.

"Excuse me," I say, turning and pretending I just noticed him. "Oh, good, you work here. Where can I find pregnancy tests?"

That question causes him to flush bright red and he stammers out an aisle number before he spins and walks away as fast as he can. I stay standing in the same spot, willing myself not to be a coward and to go and get this over with. It turns out that's easier said than done.

"Miss, can I help you with something?" A man I take to be manager level asks from behind me.

"Nope, just procrastinating," I reply, smiling at my own answer. "Wish me luck."

Leaving him looking absolutely bewildered, I go to locate the tests I came in for and decide on two different kinds before grabbing a bottle of water on the way to the check-out line.

Without being asked, the cashier points me in the direction of the bathroom as she's handing me my change and I almost ask her how frequently she's witnessed customers' *moment of truth*, but I hardly think the people in line behind me want to be held hostage because I'm too scared to go and take this stupid test.

I don't even need it honestly. I'm absolutely certain I'm pregnant.

Taking a deep breath, I follow the direction of the woman's finger and march to my future, gulping the bottle of water on the way.

Once the whole peeing on stick thing is complete, I slide the test back into the box and decide to try the ice cream store I had seen across the street. I'm barely five feet out the door when I walk into a solid wall of muscle.

Startled, I start to squeak out an apology, but immediately feel a hand around my mouth just as my eyes connect with the face that towers above me.

It's my cousin, Tober, which immediately makes my knees go weak because that means that our other cousin, Felix is undoubtedly the man behind me as they hurry me into the backseat of a waiting Cadillac.

In less than a minute, I've been shoved into a really luxurious sedan and Tober is getting into the driver's seat, where he carefully buckles up and checks his mirrors as Felix sighs in frustration.

"Every fucking time, Tober?" he nearly growls that question to our somewhat *special* cousin.

"It's been a long time, Tober. How are you doing?" I ask him, managing to keep the panic out of my voice and make it sound like we're just catching up.

"I'm doing good, Piper. Thank you for asking," he replies, smiling at me in the rear-view mirror. "Oh, could you put your seat belt on? It makes me uncomfortable when my passengers aren't safe."

"I appreciate your concern, but I'll be…" With one hand on the door release, I stop talking when I realize they must have engaged the child safety locks.

"I'm sorry, Piper, but you have to come to Vegas

with us," Tober's deep voice sounds apologetic as he patiently waits for me to buckle up.

"Just drive already, you idiot." Felix, being his exact opposite in every way, slaps him over the head before turning to me. "You sit there and keep your mouth shut."

"Are you alright, Tober?" I stubbornly ask, after loudly snapping the seat belt into place.

"Thank you, Piper," his voice conveys what his words don't. That this is par for the course with Felix and that it hurts him emotionally each time.

Tober's use of my name tells me that they were looking for me, and the only reason they would come after me now is if they need leverage over Paige, or if she had done something colossally stupid.

I decide that Paige deserves the benefit of the doubt and continue thinking through how to extract myself from their company.

Leaning forward, I see my purse sitting between my two cousins and wonder how long before I'll be able to get my hands on it. I would kind of like to see the results of the pregnancy test for myself.

Thinking about my best play here, I remember that I was supposed to check in with Me'ansome today. When I don't there could be two possible outcomes. The first is that he thinks that I'm throwing in the towel on our relationship, the other is that he'll be worried enough to have someone track my cell phone's location. That leaves a little too much to chance, in my estimation, so my best bet is to figure out how to get Tober to help me out.

"Tober, I always thought you would go to work on a ranch, like you used to talk about," I say, making small talk and ignoring Felix's glare.

"I wanted to and I found a place that would have me. It was a camp for special needs kids. They had year-round positions on account of the horses. Ma said I had to be a driver though, which meant I couldn't go," Tober tells me and continues talking about the place even after Felix turns up the radio.

"Hmm, and are you still living back in Louisiana?" I ask him, getting a loud sigh from the gentle giant as he turns down the radio.

"No, Felix wants to live in Vegas and because I drive for him, I have to live in Vegas. I don't like it there though. Too many people. Rude people and strange ones."

"I'm sorry to hear that, Tober. You must make good money though, as a chauffeur in Vegas?" I try to sound innocent but know that I oversold it when Felix turns on me.

"You say one more word and you'll ride the rest of the way in the trunk. And you," Felix turns on Tober. "Chatty Cathy, I've told you, no one wants to hear anything out of your mouth so keep what little mind you have on the road."

This time, when Tober's eyes meet mine in the rear-view mirror, beside the apology I see in them, I also notice a spark of a question. I can only hope I hit a nerve when I alluded to his salary.

I may have walked away from my family a long time ago, but I am certain of two things. How they feel about money and how they felt about having a child with less than average intelligence. My guess is that Tober gets a room at someone's house, food, and a little walking around money.

Tober is as kindhearted as they come, but he would be too frightened to stand up to Felix without a really big reason. For now, there's nothing for me to do but sit back and wait for a time that I can give Tober that reason.

It's nearly dark when I wake up, just as we're pulling out of a drive-thru.

"Don't worry, I got you something to eat, Piper," Tober assures me when he sees me twisting to look back in the hopes that I can signal someone or even see where we are.

"I'm getting a room for the night over there," Felix tells me, pointing down the road to a cluster of motels. "You're going to sit quietly back there while I go into the office, then we'll drive right up to the entrance to the room and if you make a stink, I'll knock you the fuck out."

I bite my tongue on a comment about the size of his *manhood* and Tober looks relieved while Felix smirks at me.

"See that, college girl here is the smart one," he says, knocking his cousin's shoulder like they're best buddies.

I wait until he goes into the motel office before I start in on Tober.

"Hey, don't look at me or he'll think we're talking, but do you have my purse by any chance?" I ask him and after a moment I get a nod.

"I put it on the floor down here because the phone kept vibrating and I didn't want Felix to notice it. He probably would have thrown it out the window and it's so hard getting your pictures back. At least with the old phone they gave me."

"Oh! Thank you for thinking of that," I say, smiling at him in the mirror before I give him very clear instructions. "Actually, could you reach inside of it and pull out, well, this is embarrassing, but there are two boxes that have pregnancy tests. One of them is already opened, I just really want to know the result. I peed on it earlier, so maybe use a napkin from the fast food place."

"Are you trying to trick me, Piper?" he asks me after letting another precious moment go by.

"No, Tober. I fell in love with someone and I think I'm pregnant now," I tell him, completely sincere and kick myself for the fact that the first time I say that out loud is to my cousin and not Me'ansome.

"Were you with him in Spokane? Because I didn't see anyone else with you and Felix will get mad if I left someone who would call the police on us," he asks, focusing on a detail that's trivial to me, but important to him.

"No, he's back in Utah," I explain. "I didn't even think about being pregnant when I left."

"Why did you leave him if you love him?" Tober's simple question rips me apart.

"I was scared of loving him because of how our family is," I answer him quietly and honestly, turning my head away when I feel my eyes flood with tears.

Felix suddenly slams his hand on the hood of the Cadillac and signals Tober to follow him. Once the sedan has been very carefully reversed into the indicated spot, the two of them talk for a moment near the trunk before Felix goes in to check the room.

"Here's what is going to happen," he starts talking the moment Tober propels me through the door and points to the bathroom behind him. "You can pee now, then eat—damn it, Tober, go back out to the car and get the food—I'll let you go to the bathroom one more time after you eat, then you're parking your ass in that chair overnight. And I'm zip-tying your wrist to the table leg so you don't think you can go wandering off tonight.

I nod, just happy that he put the bathroom at the top of his list, and dart past him to take care of business. Naturally, he had already checked the cramped room to make sure there wasn't a window and I'm not disappointed because he probably would have stood over me if there was.

After dinner, each of the guys settle into one of the double beds and with reruns of some sitcom playing on the ancient TV, they fall asleep. Or at least, I thought they both had.

With more finesse than I thought he would be capable of, Tober slides off of his bed and before I know it, he has disengaged the locks and snuck outside.

Without me.

I sigh to myself, wondering what he's up to as I keep an eye on Felix as he snores away.

Tober doesn't acknowledge me when he returns, so I frantically start trying to come up with another plan.

After a fitful few hours of sleep, Felix wakes me when he cuts the zip-tie off of my wrist; barely giving me time to use the bathroom before he's wrapping his arm around my bicep and hauling me out to shove me into the open back door of the sedan that's already running.

Then I hear a very loud click.

"Seat belt! Now!" Tober screams, his eyes are wide open and glazed with either fear or exhilaration.

Felix's hands slap against the side of the Cadillac as we go screeching out of the parking spot.

I can't help but to look back at Felix and instantly know that our faces are wearing identical expressions of shock.

"Way to go, cousin!" I clap my hands and laugh with joy over our escape.

"Put your seat belt on, Piper," he responds, looking mildly ill.

I immediately comply, knowing how important it is to him.

"Where are we going?" I calmly ask once my heart rate has calmed down.

"To Parker," he answers, his face finally starting to relax as he pulls onto the highway. "I went out to check your pregnancy test and I noticed that you had a lot of missed messages from him, so I called him and told him Felix kidnapped you because his ma told him to."

"Tober, can you please tell me exactly what you two talked about?" I try to keep my voice calm even though my heart is beating out of my chest.

"Sure, I told him you loved him and you didn't really want to leave him. I also told him that it wouldn't be good for you or your baby if we brought you to Vegas," he cheerfully recites what he said to Parker and I suddenly feel nauseous.

"Can I see the test?"

"Oh, sure. Here's your purse. I just need to keep your phone plugged in because Parker said he would call this morning and the battery is really low. I didn't charge it last night."

I open my mouth to ask him how he accessed my phone but the sight of the positive test distracts me and a sob flies out of me. "What did he say when you told him I was pregnant?"

"A lot of cuss words."

Me'ansome

That's it. I think to myself when Piper doesn't pick up my call or respond to my text.

Some part of me kept thinking this day would come, but it still fucking hurts. I should have been ready for this.

"You ready to go?" Tin asks from the doorway and I nod, putting on my sunglasses and look around to make sure I didn't leave anything behind.

We were able to wrap up our negotiations earlier than planned so I thought it'd be worth it to surprise Piper. We're about five hours south of the border and will stay in Tucson tonight before continuing home tomorrow.

"How's Piper?" Tin asks, his sideway glance tells me he's already guessed.

"Don't know." With that, I walk ahead of him waving off the manager's broken English as I head straight to my ride.

"Shit happens," Tin tells me, before turning on his bike. "Try her again in bit."

I almost miss the second half of his comment

over the roar of his engine, when it breaks the silence of the sleepy street around us. I shrug, not wanting to commit, but think it's a solid point.

By the time we hit the U.S. border, I had called her three more times and sent texts to her once we stopped for the night.

I decide to stop moping around the room and go meet Tin at his favorite bar down the road, when my phone rings. My heart leaps when Piper's name and picture pop up on the home screen.

"Piper, are you alright?" I ask without preamble, trying to keep my voice calm.

"Are you the man Piper's in love with?" Comes another man's voice and I have to reach out, steadying myself against the wall. "Because it isn't her fault she couldn't answer her phone."

His words barely making sense to me. "Who the fuck is this?"

"Hi, I'm Tober. I'm her cousin. My other cousin, Felix, and I had to kidnap her. He isn't very nice and I don't think it would be good for her in Vegas. I don't like it there at all, there's too much traffic."

I think I'm suffocating or having a stroke. I close my eyes and all I can see is darkness with white flashes of light jumping out at me as I deeply inhale and exhale while trying to make sense of his words.

"Put Piper on the phone. I want to know what's happening," I slowly grind out those words.

"I can't. Felix will find out." This Tober guy sounds pretty concerned about that. "Piper told me she fell in love and when I came out to see if she was telling me the truth about her pregnancy test, I saw all the missed calls from you."

"What did the test say?" I ask, wondering if I'll die before the riddle of this call is resolved.

"She's pregnant! Congratulations!" Tober sounds excited for a moment. "I thought I said that before, but I get confused sometimes. I don't think being in Vegas with our family would be good for her or the baby."

Fuck, holding onto the wall, I get close enough to the bed and just lie back on it.

"You can't say all those things when the baby comes." Tober's voice sounds a little off when he makes me realize I've been swearing up a blue streak.

"I'm going to be a dad again," I whisper.

"Maybe I can drive Piper to you, but then I can't go back to Vegas," he tells me. "Or Louisiana. They would find me there too."

"Tober, is it? I need you to answer some questions for me, alright? I promise to help you start over wherever you want to go," I vow to this cousin of hers.

In the next ten minutes, I feel like I've aged a decade, but Tober and I work out a plan. After having him repeat it back to me a couple of times, I let him go back to their room with strict instructions not to communicate with Piper, because the whole plan will implode if Felix gets wind of anything.

"Hey, did she really say she loves me?" I ask, feeling like I'm in junior high.

"Yes. She said she loves you, that's why I thought you'd help us."

"Thanks, man. I'll see you tomorrow."

The line disconnects and I take a deep breath while I consider what I'm more excited about. Piper telling this guy she loves me or being a dad again.

Getting ahold of Tin, I quickly realize he had a few too many shots to be driving through the night, but not enough that he didn't encourage me to get a little rest myself.

I figure that even with the four hours we got, we'll still be in good shape considering that they would be sleeping. An early morning call to my Knights gets them rolling up the interstate with their eyes on the lookout for the Cadillac that Tober had described.

My second call is entirely too brief and with my voice piping through the sound system of the car Tober is driving, I don't say anything I truly want to. Piper's words are also guarded, but I need to see her face to get a read on what she's feeling.

It's the middle of the afternoon when I see my men, riding in formation around the Caddy as it pulls off into the travel plaza and comes to a screeching halt after Piper has already thrown open her door.

Before I know it, she's in my arms again, her legs wrapped around my waist in a hold any wrestler would be proud of, I kiss her until I can't breathe.

"I heard you love me." I can't help the grin that feels like it stretches from ear to ear.

"I had hoped to be the first one to tell you that," she laughs, rolling her eyes before burying her face into my neck. "I would have also liked knowing the test results before Tober did, but we can't always get what we want."

"Oh, no, Piper. I got what I want," I say, tilting her chin up so I can kiss her again; only looking up when someone clears their throat and I look over at a man who's larger than my son-in-law.

"Piper, there are rules. You have to have your seat

belt on when I'm driving and you can't open the door when the car is moving. I let you move into the front seat that one time, but I won't break that rule again."

Shifting Piper to my left hip, I walk to within a few feet of the man. The closer I get, the stiller he becomes, keeping his attention squarely on the ground in front of him.

"Tober?" I ask, extending my right hand to shake his. Black eyes meet mine for an instant before they study my hand, taking a few more moments before he reaches out to shake it. "Thank you for what you've done. I owe you everything."

"You're not mad at me?" he asks, his timid voice irreconcilable to his size.

"You're not going to kidnap my Old Lady again, are you?" My question gets a gasp from Piper and a puzzled expression from Tober.

"I don't think she's older than you," he says, looking between our faces.

"Will you come home with us, Tober?" Piper gently asks him, reaching out to squeeze his shoulder. "You could stay until you figure out what you want to do."

"Is that alright with you?" His eyes finally meet mine for more than a few seconds and I nod. "Thank you."

As he goes to get back into his Caddy to fill up the tank, Piper taps her finger on my nose.

"Ol' Lady, huh?"

"Yeah, I don't think I can survive you leaving me again. Or getting kidnapped. I'm keeping you, that's final."

"In that case, you should know I come with some baggage," Piper tells me, resting her head on my shoulder as I walk to my Harley.

"Anything serious?"

"My family is completely warped. My sister is in the wind. And, I'm knocked up," she counts each item off on a finger before dramatically sighing and waving her hand in the air. "For starters, at least."

"Fuck your family. We'll find your sister. And we'll be incredible parents. Now, if you need to use the bathroom get to it, because I want to go crawl into bed for a few days and I don't sleep too good without you."

Hours later, after getting Tober settled in down the hall from us and sharing a much needed shower with Piper. I hold her sleeping form in my arms and pray that I'm up to the task of fatherhood again.

EPILOGUE

Me'ansome – *A couple of months later*

"And your mom?" Ransom asks me.

"I reached out to her when I was about nineteen. That was when I found out that Parson had left for the States the year before. Fetch took my request seriously and had been looking after her from the moment I had left." I reach out to twist the cap off the new beer Axel brought over. "Mark's doing well, he stayed in Truro and has a high-end barber shop he calls, Jabba the Cutt. We always did love those movies."

"Do you think you'll go back to visit one day?" Piper asks me. Joey and Ransom exchange a glance, knowing more of the story than she does.

"Nah, this is my home," I tell her, rubbing her

lower back. The groan she lets out instantly hardens my dick, and I shift forward to press it against her ass.

Joey lets out a snort, which is quickly answered by Ransom's snicker, letting me know that everyone can see through my intentions. I try to glare at them, but my eyes are suddenly too moist to relay mock anger.

This is what it's all about.

My children are back with me and acting like they've known each other their whole lives, while I hold Piper tight in my arms and start to feel more confident about being a dad again.

For everything that went wrong the first time around, this time is going to be a breeze.

Piper

"Damn it!" I groan, looking at my phone after a particularly grueling Zoom meeting.

I'd been trying to get ahold of Paige for weeks now, or more precisely, get to see her in person but she's been determined to complete whatever job our mother had tasked her with.

Of course, it's the one time she has tried to call me back.

I scroll through her text messages as I hit redial and am somewhat relieved to at least have her location now.

"Hey, don't be mad at me," she starts talking as soon as she answers the call. Paige doesn't sound stressed, but I wish we could have a normal conversation.

"I can't remember the last time you answered the phone like a normal person," I muse.

"If I promise to work on that, will you please come pick me up?" Now I can hear a hint of stress in her voice, so I sit up straighter. "I dropped a pin where I need you to get me, how soon can you be here?"

Shit. Shit. Shit.

"Um, let me figure that out and I'll text you. Don't do anything crazy in the meanwhile, Paige!" My voice hits a higher octane than normal as I walk to the kitchen in search of Me'ansome.

"Cross my heart," she answers before disconnecting.

"Parker! It's Paige, we need to go and get her. How soon can we, get to…" I look down at the map and rather than explain the area on the outskirts of Los Angeles, I just show it to him.

"You're not going anywhere," he growls, reaching for my phone. "Actually, let me call Tin. He's probably close to Vegas now and can swing to get her before he heads north to Fresno."

I breathe a sigh of relief, hurrying off to the bathroom, believing that Tin is probably one of the few people who will, calmly, deal with whatever trouble Paige has found herself in.

Yes, I think to myself. If ever there was anyone to pick Paige up and bring her back to me without any high jinks, it's Tin.

"It's all set," Me'ansome tells me from the hallway. "I used your phone to text her the time he gave me."

He hands my cell back to me, looking a little sheepish about sending a message on my behalf but considering the extra weight I have around my bladder nowadays, I barely glance at it.

"Are you busy?" I ask, reaching out to take his hand.

He smiles and shakes his head, "What'd you have in mind?"

"There was something else I was hoping you could help me with," I answer coyly. "In the bedroom."

"Do I need my toolbox? I'll just grab it from the

garage," he deadpans and starts to turn away from me.

"You have all the tools you need, old man," I assure him.

THE END

THANK YOU

To Sapphire Knight, I appreciate that you didn't take a restraining order out against me when I constantly 'checked in' about getting into MMM19 and I'm so excited to be a part of this signing also. Without this collaboration, Me'ansome's story wouldn't have been told for a long time. XO

To Elizabeth M. Karr, although we've never met or spoken directly—thank you so much for sharing your memories of Cornwall and a bit of your family history with me, through your son, Marty. I enjoyed hearing about the area so much, that I hope to visit it someday.

To Tina Workman, thank you for adopting me at my first MMM and making my world so much brighter.

To Erin Toland, my long-suffering editor, thank you for all your kindnesses and endless patience.

To Brenda Keller, your covers are almost as beautiful as your smile! Thank you for all you do behind the scenes.

To Marty, thank you for helping me add a little bit of you to 'your character'.

ADDITIONAL WORKS FROM M. MERIN

Northern Grizzlies MC Series:

Jasper (Book 1)

Flint (Book 2)

Gunner (Book 3)

Charlie (Book 4)

Michaels (Book 5)

Betsy (Book 6)

Shade (Book 7)

Chains: Northern Grizzlies MC Short I

Wrench: Northern Grizzlies MC Short II

Royal Bastards MC, Flagstaff Chapter:

Axel (Book 1)

Declan (Book 2)

Diesel (Book 3)

Snowed In, A Royal Bastard Surprise (Book 4)

Wolfman (Book 5)

Also Available:

Black Hills Shifters Books 2 & 4

His Touch

Ever After Series: Dark Ever After (Book 1)

& Julia's Journey (Book 2)

Molotov Brothers: The Reluctant King (Book 1)

Kal: A Rogue Enforcers Novella

The Weight of Blood (A Cuffed and Pinched Duet)

MMM Mayhem Makers Collaboration

Me'ansome: Grave Knights MC (Book 1)

Tin: Grave Knights MC (Book 2)

www.ingramcontent.com/pod-product-compliance
Lightning Source LLC
Chambersburg PA
CBHW050853180626
46814CB00007B/2748